P. Sergieenko

How Count L. M. Tolstoy Lives and Works

P. Sergieenko

How Count L. M. Tolstoy Lives and Works

ISBN/EAN: 9783337319526

Printed in Europe, USA, Canada, Australia, Japan

Cover: Foto ©Raphael Reischuk / pixelio.de

More available books at **www.hansebooks.com**

How Count L. N. Tolstoy Lives and Works

By

P. A. SERGYEENKO

Translated from the Russian

By

ISABEL F. HAPGOOD

NEW YORK: 46 East 14th Street
THOMAS Y. CROWELL & COMPANY
BOSTON: 100 Purchase Street

HOW COUNT TOLSTOY LIVES AND WORKS

CHAPTER I

ABOUT four o'clock in the afternoon, in the winter of 1892, I was sitting with my friends the A.'s, who had arrived in Moscow on the previous evening from their estate in the south. Several other guests besides myself were seated at the tea-table engaged in a lively conversation about one of Lyeff Tolstoy's latest works.

Out of doors a fine snow was falling and in the room the twilight was gathering.

Just as the discussion had reached its height, a gaunt old man, of medium stature and with the typical face of the Russian peasant, entered the room. He wore a short, sheepskin coat and tall felt boots. As he entered he said, "Good-afternoon," removed his felt cap, and began to unwind from his throat a woolen scarf.

From the table where we sat, we could not see the door plainly, and the A.'s stared with curiosity and surprise at the newcomer.

Suddenly the hostess's face beamed with delight, and she said, in a drawling voice: —

"Lyeff Nikolaevitch! how do you do?"

All rose to their feet.

It was Count L. N. Tolstoy. He untied his scarf, and, with a brisk, youthful movement, threw off his fur coat, casting sharp glances about as he did so in search of a place to lay it.

I beheld L. N. Tolstoy for the first time, and, involuntarily, riveted my eyes upon him. He was clad in a dark gray flannel blouse with a wide, turn-down collar, displaying his sinewy neck at the curves of the head. He was breathing rather fast from his walk in the cold air, and his gray hair lay in damp, tumbled locks upon his temples. He had an alert, wide-awake air, held himself upright, and moved with quick, short steps, hardly bending his knees, which suggested the motion of a man sliding upon ice. He appeared neither older nor younger than his age — he was then sixty-four — and produced the impression of a well-preserved, energetic peasant. And his face, also, was a true peasant's face: simple, rustic, with a broad nose, a weather-beaten skin, and thick, overhanging brows, from beneath which small, keen, gray eyes peered sharply forth.

But the expression of his eyes was unusual, and involuntarily attracted attention. In them seemed to be concentrated all the vivid tokens of Tolstoy's personality; and he who has not seen those eyes flash and blaze, who has not seen them suddenly acquire a sort of boring and penetrating character, cannot possess a full conception of L. N. Tolstoy's external appearance.

Although the majority of his portraits reproduce his external features with considerable success, so that L. N. Tolstoy may instantly be recognized from them, yet not one of them gives a clear idea of the core of his personality, not one transmits those fountains of light hidden in the man, which, when they are reflected upon his countenance at certain moments, illuminate it with the gleam of the inner life. This defect in the portraits of L. N. Tolstoy must be charged, in part, to his account. Because of the qualities of his vivacious, impatient nature, he presents a difficult subject for the artist. The artist must *carry in himself* a certain engraved expression, and never seek it again at the time of actual work.

After he had hung up his fur coat, L. N. Tolstoy approached us and began to exchange greetings. In spite of his modest attire, one instantly divines in Lyeff Nikolaevitch a man of the highest society, — well-bred, with polished, unconstrained manners.

We were introduced to each other.

L. N. Tolstoy bent down slightly, as though trying to scrutinize my face, and said courteously: —

"Pray excuse me for not having written to you in regard to your article which you sent to me."

Several months previously I had sent to L. N. Tolstoy my article about a certain priest, who was exterminating drunkenness among the masses by his sermons.

In this connection I had written to L. N. Tolstoy a few lines about the sympathetic personality of the priest. I was pleasantly surprised that, amid his extensive occupations, he had forgotten neither my modest work nor my name, and I said: —

"You probably had your reasons for so doing."

"Yes, yes, you are right," he replied, seating himself and pointing me to a place beside him. "There is a very great deal to say on the subject with which you dealt in your article. I had no leisure at the time, and I made up my mind that when I came to Moscow I would manage to call upon you and talk it over."

And, picking up a pencil which was lying on the table and swiftly twirling it about in his fingers, Lyeff Nikolaevitch began to talk about the thing which then interested me most. He talked without constraint, cleverly and picturesquely, in the same richly colored language in which he writes, easily reasoning and easily discussing the most complicated situations. It was difficult to answer him. He seemed to have at his disposal a whole arsenal of the clearest, boldest, most original, and utterly unexpected arguments, with pertinent comparisons and humorous interpolations, which evoked involuntary laughter. Yet, nevertheless, I could not in the least agree with some of his positions, and I tried to reply. He refuted my objections on the instant, without ceasing to twirl the pencil, and hastily brought forward his own ideas, which breathed forth ingenuity, power, and passion. The conversation at last became general and turned upon other themes.

The corridor servant brought the bubbling samovar. Madame A. offered Lyeff Nikolaevitch tea, but he categorically refused it, and cast a hostile glance at the battery of preserve jars which stood on the table; then he turned his gaze to the good-natured face of the hostess, and his stern features softened. He began, in a friendly tone, to talk to her about her work in wool (she had been engaged in preparing yarn during the conversation), and about the vegetarian kitchen which Madame A. was planning to build in Moscow. On encountering my glance, Lyeff Nikolaevitch began to talk about the advantage of vegetable food, and advised me to leave off eating meat; then he appealed to Mr. A. concerning some new influences in the realm of law (A. is a jurist-theorist, absorbed in juridical science), and then, gradually, he entered into conversation with each person present about the thing which most interested them, evidently fearing that he might omit some one or other from his attention.

The conversation turned upon one of his sons, who, at the moment, was seeking an estate, for purchase.

"Lyeff Nikolaevitch, tell your son that when he has decided upon any estate, he is to apply to me. I will give him some indispensable hints, otherwise he may commit follies."

Lyeff Nikolaevitch shrugged his shoulders.

"Why prevent him? The more follies he commits, the better it will be for him."

I did not understand the sense of these words, and asked, "Why will it be the better for him?"

"Because the sooner he sets his teeth on edge with estates, and at last convinces himself, from his personal experience, that nothing good will come from this, the quicker will he attain to the comprehension of the fact that the only person for whom it is profitable to hold land is the man who tills it himself."

"Very good, if it does turn out so," I remarked, "but failures do not always lead us to the truth. Sometimes they merely enrage a man, and spoil his character."

L. N. Tolstoy darted a sharp glance from beneath his gray, beetling brows.

"My son is not in that path," he ejaculated abruptly.

And it seemed to me that a sort of shadow came between us.

Having exhausted the subject of the purchase of an estate, Lyeff Nikolaevitch laid the pencil on the table, and clasped his hands, with the fingers interlocking. His overhanging brows drooped still lower, and his face assumed a locked-up expression. The conversation evidently had wearied him, and he only listened to his interlocutor out of politeness. When the latter had finished, Lyeff Nikolaevitch asked the hour, and rose.

But before his departure a characteristic episode took place. In the course of conversation with one of the persons present, Lyeff Nikolaevitch mentioned Bertha Suttner's famous book, *Die Waffen nieder!* and said, "Of course you have read the book?"

The man nodded his head in assent. But his conscience must have tormented him for telling Lyeff Nikolaevitch an untruth, and he stammered out:—

"Lyeff Nikolaevitch, I really am acquainted with the contents of that book, *Away with Arms!* But I have not yet read the book itself."

L. N. Tolstoy changed the subject, and began to take leave. But it seemed to me that he was greatly touched by his interlocutor's confession, and that he fully appreciated the significance of the conquest over himself which the man had made.

Lyeff Nikolaevitch put on his short fur coat, hooked it up tightly, and putting himself to rights in peasant fashion — with a movement of the shoulders — he began to don and praise the mittens of goat's wool given to him by Madame A.; then he made a general salute, and left the room with accelerated steps.

He was in haste to get home to dinner, and he had several versts to traverse before he reached Weaver's Lane, where he lives. He does not like to ride in cabs, and has recourse to them only in exceptional cases.

CHAPTER II

A WEEK after my first meeting with L. N. Tolstoy, I availed myself of his invitation, and about eight o'clock in the evening drove, in company with the A.'s, to Dolgo-Khamovnitcheskiy Pereulok (Long-Weaver's Lane), where the Tolstoys live in winter. They occupy a separate two-story wooden house, belonging to one of Lyeff Nikolaevitch's sons, Lyeff Lvovitch.

The small, isolated two-story house to which we drove up was situated in a courtyard, and stood out as a dark mass against the whitish background of the ancient garden, sprinkled with hoar frost. The outer principal door, and the second door, with a stiff spring, were not fastened. Through ignorance I let this second door go, and it produced a deafening bang, which brought out a courteous lackey in dress-suit, who began to help us off with our outer wraps.

The A.'s were, in part, acquainted with the ways of the house at the Tolstoys', and thought that no one but ourselves would be there that evening.

But in the anteroom, on the cloak-rack, there were many outer garments, and to the right, upon the wall-chests and the pier-tables, lay a motley collection of all sorts of caps, fur caps and uniform caps. The servant softly inquired of us, Whom were we come to visit, the Count or the Countess?

The A.'s said that we had come to see the Count. The servant announced us, and, a moment later, returned with an invitation from the Count.

On the landing of the broad staircase, with one turn, one of Lyeff Nikolaevitch's daughters met us. She greeted us unconstrainedly, like intimate friends, and conducted us through the large hall where sat several ladies and gentlemen. From the hall we entered a narrow corridor, descended several steps, and found ourselves in a small, low-studded room, with an iron pipe extending across it close to the ceiling. This arrangement of the pipe is due to one of L. N. Tolstoy's acquaintances; its peculiarity consists in the fact that, with the aid of a lamp, it ventilates and, in part, heats the working cabinet capitally.

Lyeff Nikolaevitch was sitting at a small writing-table, with his foot tucked up under him, engaged in writing something by the light of a candle. At our appearance he rose, and began to exchange courteous greeting, sometimes raising his hand on high, and lowering it again with a gentle movement; then he gave us seats, and began to talk about the book which lay open before him, and which he was reading after dinner. It was a new French book on social questions. Its style pleased him, as did some individual ideas in it, but, on the whole, he did not find it satisfactory, and he began to explain precisely why it did not satisfy him.

The solitary candle left the study rather dark, and the corners were submerged in gloom. I involuntarily cast a glance around the room, where so many immortal images had had their birth and been created.

It was a small, almost square chamber wholly without decorations, with a low ceiling and broad windows, which looked out on the garden. Beside one window stood a small, plain table covered with papers, and a half-empty bookcase.

Lyeff Nikolaevitch's library is at Yasnaya Polyana, and in Moscow he keeps only reference books dealing with the subject on which he is working. In another corner of the study was a broad divan, covered with oil-cloth, and by the side of the divan stood a small, round table and a few arm-chairs, and this constituted the entire furniture of the study, which recalled in its simplicity the workroom of Pascal, for whom L. Tolstoy cherishes a profound respect in general; and in many points he appears as the follower of the French philosopher in the matter of habits, as well as in the realm of thought. For some time I could not get my bearings, or decide at what height from the earth we were, because the road to the study was rather complicated.

Afterward I learned that Lyeff Nikolaevitch's study lies, as it were, between heaven and earth. The fact is that when, in the beginning of the '80's, the whole house was in process of being rebuilt, Lyeff Nikolaevitch did not wish to yield his study as a sacrifice to the god of luxury, and assured the Countess that many extremely useful workers lived and labored in incomparably worse quarters than he. The study was left in its previous condition, but this spoiled the side façade of the house facing the garden. On the other hand, as regards quiet and tranquillity, the study was the gainer thereby. Far removed from the street noises, and the dwelling-rooms, it is always filled with that stillness which is conducive to meditation. In the spacious, ancient garden, upon which the study windows look out, a skating-place is arranged in winter; and there, among other things, is situated the well of pure, healthful water, whence Lyeff Nikolaevitch, for lack of other physical labor at hand, draws water and drives it in a cask for the household needs.

Lyeff Nikolaevitch was in an excellent frame of mind. Over his finely modeled lips, unconcealed by mustaches, flitted a smile every moment, accompanying humorous interpolations.

Before I knew him, judging from his portraits, I had always regarded Lyeff Nikolaevitch as a man locked up within himself, and rather gloomy. This is not true. He is very sociable, talkative, likes a jest, highly prizes humor, and readily has recourse to it.

During the conversation in the study, one of Lyeff Nikolaevitch's daughters entered and said: —

"Papa, N. has come, and is waiting for you, in order to read the article he promised."

Lyeff Nikolaevitch rose and addressed us: —

"Do not go away until I return. Here are the new journals. Here is an interesting manuscript of a common working-man. But I must go and listen to the nonsense which N. has written."

I was rather surprised by Lyeff Nikolaevitch's prediction concerning the work of N., who is considered one of the most talented of Russian writers.

About forty minutes later, Lyeff Nikolaevitch returned, accompanied by two new visitors, and was visibly excited, somewhat suggesting a man who has escaped from captivity.

"I thought so," he began in a rather vexed tone,—"that N. would regale us with twaddle. But his new nonsense is utterly absurd. At the same time, it is evident that he has expended not a little exertion and thought upon it. And what an overwhelming phenomenon this is, in fact!" proceeded Lyeff Nikolaevitch, in a sorrowful tone. "If it were not a sin, I should sometimes like to say, in reproach: 'O Lord, why dost Thou reveal much to one man, so that it is plainer to him, than that twice two makes four? And from other men Thou concealest everything. And in all their being there is not so much as one tiny crack through which Thy light can penetrate?'"

We heard the rustle of a gown at the door, and Countess Sophia Andreevna, Lyeff Nikolaevitch's wife, entered the study with light, swift tread. She had come to invite her husband's guests up-stairs, to the "big" tea, so called to distinguish it from the "children's" tea.

Countess Sophia Andreevna, Bers by birth, is sixteen years younger than her famous husband. At the time of which I speak, she was forty-eight years of age. In spite of the fact that she has had thirteen children,[1] her aspect is still very youthful and full of life. She has an open, expressive countenance, with vivacious, fearless eyes, which she constantly brings near to the objects at which she is looking. At her very first words, one feels her straightforward nature. In her manners there is not even a shadow of truckling to suit the tone of any one whomsoever, but her own individual note is always audible.

She cordially invited us all to tea, and, chatting vivaciously with Madame A. about some domestic question, conducted us up-stairs.

[1] She told me *fifteen*.—I. F. H.

And when she walked, her still beautiful head half turned, when she addressed her husband with the word *Lyévotchka*, or interjected into the conversation some remark, one immediately felt that here reigned, if not harmony, at least complete independence of relations, and that each person had his own independent position.

The spacious, lofty hall which we entered was, also, bare of decoration. Almost in the middle of the room stood a long, broad table, covered with a white tablecloth (prepared for tea), and a row of chairs. On the right side of the entrance to the hall stood a grand piano, and a small divan with an oval table. All the furniture was ancient, of mahogany. This constituted the entire decoration. There were neither pictures, nor rugs, nor soft furniture.

But the room did not appear either empty or neglected. Rather than that, a certain indefinable, noble simplicity could be felt in everything. Nothing, in any direction, stood forth in an angle, or thrust itself into notice. On the contrary, the furniture and the hostess and the guests all had a certain peculiar easy and artless character.

At the end of the table a nickel-plated samovar was singing, and cups, cream, and cold rolls were standing. From the adjoining room, where a richer furnishing was visible, youthful voices, peals of laughter, and the sounds of stringed instruments were audible.

The Tolstoys have a very large family, and a vast circle of acquaintances. At the time in question, Lyeff Nikolaevitch's family consisted of six sons and three daughters. The young generation were constantly drawing about them their comrades, relatives, and friends, in consequence of which, in the Tolstoys' house, one always received the impression that a performance of amateur theatricals had been appointed there and that a whole flower-garden of young people were preparing for this event, filling the entire house with noisy animation in which Lyeff Nikolaevitch also occasionally takes part. Especially if any amusement is started which demands exercise, endurance, and agility, L. N. will, ever and anon, glance at the players and share heartily in their successes and failures; often, too, he cannot restrain himself, and mingles in the game, displaying so much youthful fervor and suppleness of muscle that one often grows envious in watching him. Moreover, L. N. Tolstoy has still another characteristic peculiarity: whatever he does, whether he runs a race with the young people, or sews shoes, or seats himself on his bicycle, he never, in any situation, *is ridiculous*. After introducing us to the other guests Lyeff Nikolaevitch betook himself to the oval table. His appearance evoked a noticeable animation, and, like a magnet, began to attract people to him. The Countess sat down to the samovar, and, chatting vivaciously, began to pour out the tea into large, thick cups.

Lyeff Nikolaevitch drank no tea, but later on ate some thin oatmeal porridge which he often substitutes for tea and supper. He was no longer the same man as in the study. Charm and mirth seemed to have fallen from him, and it even seemed as though he had grown somewhat older since he had come from the study into the hall. When he is fatigued, or is displeased with anything, his cheeks sink in and his face assumes a rather gloomy character which is the one chiefly reproduced in his portraits.

One of those present had heard from some one that L. N. Tolstoy wished to set to work again at his *Decembrists*, and asked him about it.

"No, I have abandoned that work forever," replied Lyeff Nikolaevitch, unwillingly. A pause ensued.

". . . because I did not find therein what I sought, that is to say, what is of general interest to mankind. That whole history had no roots under it," he added, with a shade of effort in his voice, merely to avert the awkwardness of silence.

He does not like to have people catechize him about his plans.

Afterward I learned that he had written *War and Peace* accidentally, as it were, by way of an introduction to the *Decembrists*. It came about in this way.

With the intention of writing the *Decembrists*, he began to study the epoch which preceded their activity, and with that object made the acquaintance of the famous Ermoloff and visited him. The events of 1805 and the war for the Fatherland in 1812 attracted the artistic feeling of the great writer. He began to group together several episodes and, as it were, to attach them to each other with facts from his family chronicles.

And the more deeply "the exacting artist" became engrossed in the study of historical materials, the broader grew the plan of his new work, which, at last, took possession of him and occupied five years of intense mental labor. But what Lyeff Nikolaevitch has printed constitutes only a small fraction of the work which he projected and wrote. All the rough drafts of *War and Peace* came near being lost. During a severe and prolonged illness of Countess Sophia Andreevna, these papers, through the carelessness of some persons of the household, were thrown out of the storehouse and lay for several months in the ditch. Thanks alone to the indefatigable energy and solicitude of Countess S. A. Tolstoy, the precious documents were gathered up, put in order, and are now in the Rumyantzoff Muzeum, in Moscow.

After the *Decembrists*, the conversation turned upon another of L. N. Tolstoy's unfinished romances — *Peter the Great*. This work Lyeff Nikolaevitch has entirely abandoned.

"There was much in that first matter which seemed to me too confused and distant," he said. "Nevertheless, I was personally acquainted with many of the Decembrists, and could avail myself of their information. But in the other case, I should have had to invent a very great deal. But the principal point is that my study of the original sources entirely altered my view of Peter I. He lost his former interest for me."

One of those present touched on the "post-Decembrist" emancipation epoch, and mentioned the brothers Aksakoff, Katkoff, Granovsky, Hertzen, and others, with all of whom Lyeff Nikolaevitch had been personally acquainted. At the name of Hertzen Lyeff Nikolaevitch brightened up, and narrated how he had met him in London. An opinion has gained currency that L. Tolstoy does not acknowledge that Hertzen had literary gifts. This is untrue. On the contrary, it is precisely his literary gift that he prizes very highly. And when the discussion touched that question, a fervent, youthfully fresh note rang out in Lyeff Nikolaevitch's weary voice, a note which always makes its appearance with him when he speaks of any genuine gift or fine act.

"If we were to express by the relations of percentage," said he, "the influence of our writers upon society, we should obtain, approximately, the following result: Pushkin, thirty per cent; Gogol, fifteen per cent; Turgeneff, ten per cent."

L. N. Tolstoy enumerated all the prominent Russian writers, except himself, and, reckoning Hertzen's share at eighteen per cent, he said with conviction:—

"He was brilliant and profound, which is very rarely met with."

A young artist approached our table. Lyeff Nikolaevitch entered into conversation with him about his works, and passed on to art, from which he demanded, not bouquets and cupids, but service rendered to the loftiest requirements of the human spirit. He soon passed into a passionate tone, and began to talk warmly, as he did so hastily knotting and untying a bit of string which had happened to come to hand. Some one alluded to the huge picture of a certain Moscow artist.

"Well, then, take that picture," said Lyeff Nikolaevitch, excitedly. "Who wants that coarse daub, which simply reeks of the knout? I cannot endure such 'Russian' productions. And why those stupid phizes? Who is there that does not know that there are stupid phizes in the world? But art ought always to say something new, because it is the expression of the artist's inner condition, and only answers its appointed use when the artist gives us something that no one hitherto has given, and which cannot be better expressed in any other way. There is Gay's *Christ before Pilate*, — that is genuine art, although the picture is badly painted. But no one before Gay ever said it *in that way*, and it was impossible to say it by any other means, than as Gay did by his tortured Christ, and his well-fed, fat Pilate. And Christ and Pilate have always and everywhere been, and will be, exactly such persons. And see how Gay toils over his subjects! For tens of years he studied the life of Christ, and not from the external, Palestine side, like others, but from the inside. You would go to him at night, and he would be sitting with rumpled hair, on the divan, reading the Gospels. And there is no other way possible. For art is a vast, a mighty instrument."

Evidently, the young artist did not wholly agree with Lyeff Nikolaevitch, and he cautiously began to present the idea that, in art, the *how*, not the *what*, is important.

"But, assuredly, Lyeff Nikolaevitch, you recognize prayer?" he asked irresolutely.

"Of course. Is it possible to live without prayer?"

"Well, then, for the artist his picture may be a prayer. Only, one expresses it by a historical subject, another in fantastic images, a third by landscape."

"Then wall-paper must be reckoned as art," interrupted Lyeff Nikolaevitch, making a noose in the string.

"But you must admit that a certain landscape may have an ennobling effect upon the soul of man. That is to say, it may act upon his soul, and in transmission it may engender in him a good feeling or prevent his perpetrating something bad."

"And a cat which leaps from the table to the floor may prevent something," retorted Lyeff Nikolaevitch, intractably, and went on to characterize the conditions that constitute something in the nature of *false art*, which people do not need in the least.

"Nowadays, go where you will," said he, "into a book-shop, china-shop, a jeweler's shop, — everywhere there is art. And not any amateur art, but patented art, with diplomas and gold medals. Go to the theater, — and there again is art: some woman or other kicks her heels higher than her head. And this repulsive stupidity is not only not considered improper, but, on the contrary, is elevated into something first-class and so important for people, that a fixed place is even set apart for it in the newspapers, alongside the greatest events of the world. Some organs of the press have, moreover, regular appraisers, who often drive straight from the theater to the printing-office, by night, and there, instantly, amid the rumbling of the machines, write down their impressions in haste, that on the morrow the world may know exactly how, on the previous evening, Madame So-and-So kicked up her heels in such and such a theater."

"But God grant that all this may be sifted out, in time, and that good, nutritious flour may be obtained as a result," remarked one of his hearers.

"Why must I wait?" retorted Lyeff Nikolaevitch. "Even now I feel the husks in my teeth. The trouble is that no end to these husks is visible, because, day by day, they are artificially manufactured in the person of divers music and art schools, which disfigure thousands of young lives. But without these nursery-gardens of every sort of lie and routine these young lives might have been of use to mankind."

"Well, very good, Lyeff Nikolaevitch," said one of his interlocutors, "we will admit that the musical and artistic institutions which exist in Russia really are of no profit to the world. We will admit that, and mentally annihilate them. Then what institutions will you give us in place of these worthless ones?"

"What a strange claim!" ejaculated Lyeff Nikolaevitch, in amazement, shrugging his shoulders. "It's just the same as though a sick man were to come to me with a swollen face. The swollen face embarrasses him. The swollen face is a burden to him. I cure him of the swollen face. Then he turns on me: 'And what are you going to give me, in place of the swollen face?' Why, nothing is necessary in place of the swollen face."

Every one began to laugh.

A student, with a clever, sympathetic face, entered the room unconstrainedly, and politely saluted Lyeff Nikolaevitch, who returned his greeting in a friendly manner and introduced him to us. The student had just come from some meeting, where some one had read something about the French writer, Taine, who had recently died. Lyeff Nikolaevitch became interested in the student's narration, but when the latter began, with some pathos, to speak of Taine's great merits, Lyeff Nikolaevitch interrupted him.

"What are his great merits? Why, if the truth were to be told, plainly, in Russian, Taine was a tolerably dull man."

The student started, but restrained himself, and said, with a smile: —

"So you mean to say, Lyeff Nikolaevitch, that Taine was narrow on some questions."

"I mean to say exactly what I did say: that Taine was, on the whole, a narrow man, otherwise it is impossible to explain his efforts to reduce the influence of man in the history of mankind almost to a cipher, and relegate the chief *rôle* to various factors, like water, clay, and so forth. Is not that stupidity? But how about Buddha! How about Christ! Did not they change the forms of life of millions of men? For clay and water cannot progress, but only living life led by the spirit, which sheds abroad in successive aspects its influence upon the most remote ages and generations."

The student listened with respect to Lyeff Nikolaevitch, with one hand thrust under the edge of his uniform, but evidently he did not entirely agree with him. At his last words he bowed slightly, and said: —

"But anthropology proves — "

"What can be proved by anthropology which, itself, still stands in need of proof? It was invented in order to obtain the greater wages."

"You deny — "

"Wages? I never thought of such a thing."

"But, anthropology is not manufactured out of one's

own head, but deduced from facts, obtained by scientific investigators —"

"What facts? The investigator arrives on the coast, and, with the aid of a dull interpreter, inquires their ways and habits; the interpreter lies about the whole thing, and the investigator carefully writes down, and adds something or other of his own."

The student began to be agitated.

I looked at Lyeff Nikolaevitch, and I seemed to see spread out before me those stormy scenes in Nekrasoff's lodgings, which took place in the '50's, when young, impetuous Count L. Tolstoy, presenting a living embodiment of Tchatsky,[1] played in St. Petersburg literary circles the part of gadfly, and in the harshest form expressed his protests against everything which seemed to him conventional and false.

"You cannot imagine what scenes there were," relates D. B. Grigorovitch. "Oh, heavens! Turgeneff would squeak and squeak, clutch his throat with his hand, and, with the eyes of a dying gazelle, would whisper: —

"'I can endure no more. I have bronchitis.'

"'Bronchitis,' Tolstoy would growl out immediately after; 'bronchitis — is an imaginary malady — bronchitis is a mental —'

"Nekrasoff's heart died within him; he was afraid to lose both Turgeneff and Tolstoy, in whom, he instinctively felt, lay the chief strength of the *Contemporary*. He had to manœuver. All are irritated. They do not know what to say. Tolstoy is lying in the middle of the room which serves as corridor, on a morocco-covered divan, and sulking, while Turgeneff, parting the skirts of his short pea-jacket, with hands thrust into his pockets, continues to stride back and forth through all three rooms. With the object of averting a catastrophe, D. Grigorovitch approaches Tolstoy.

"'My dear Tolstoy, do not be vexed. You do not know how he values and loves you.'

"'I will not permit him to do anything to harm me,'

[1] The hero of Griboydeff's famous comedy, *The Misfortune of Wit.* — TR.

says Tolstoy, with swelling nostrils. 'Here he is marching to and fro past me, and wagging his democratic haunches.'"

I involuntarily recall that scene, when L. Tolstoy, the first time he spent the evening with Panaeff, could not restrain his tendency to disputations, and hotly began to talk of precisely the thing which D. Grigorovitch had begged him not to mention to Panaeff.

And when I gazed at Lyeff Nikolaevitch during his dispute with the student, it became clear to me precisely why he behaved so demonstratively toward Turgeneff in the literary circles of St. Petersburg.

By virtue of his nature, Lyeff Tolstoy *cannot* pass over in silence the phenomenon which he considers monstrous, just as the sea cannot remain tranquil when the wind rises. This is a property of his nature. It imparts vast strength to Lyeff Tolstoy, but, at the same time, it creates for him an inward hell, before which the tragedy of soul which Hamlet experienced must pale.

Countess Sophia Andreevna approached Lyeff Nikolaevitch, and said, in a low voice, that several of the guests wished to occupy themselves with music. Lyeff Nikolaevitch rose with alacrity, threw away the string, and, as though gliding on ice, hastily betook himself to the large table. On learning that they proposed to begin by playing Wieniawski (piano and violin), and then Beethoven (piano, violin, and violoncello), he set to work to arrange everything as soon as possible. He hunted up the music, helped to raise the lid of the piano, and when all was in readiness, he sat down, with a concentrated manner, on one side, and listened attentively to the music. At the end of each piece he rose, and, thrusting his left hand into the belt of his blouse, he walked, with body bent forward, to the performers, thanked them for the pleasure they had given him, and made subtile comments on the more successful passages.

And, as I looked at that delicate and well-bred man, from whose every word shone forth sensitiveness, it was difficult to imagine him as the vehement protester, lying with inflated nostrils on the divan, and unwilling to yield so much as an iota to one of the most inoffensive men in the world.

Lyeff Nikolaevitch's praise gave the performers great pleasure, and with visible cheerfulness they executed several more pieces at his request. Whether he did this in order to afford pleasure to his guests, or with the object of obtaining a little respite from the fatiguing conversation, or whether he yielded to his passion for music,—who knows? Perhaps all these motives were intermingled within him. But he listened with concentration, with attention, with head bowed, and gently moving the fingers of his clasped hands.

CHAPTER III

THREE weeks later I happened again to be at the Tolstoys'. Again they had many visitors, and again, after tea, began something in the nature of a concert section. One of the ladies sang. But, evidently, the singing displeased the boys. They went into the adjoining room and made a noise there. Lyeff Nikolaevitch lost his patience and went after the boys.

"Are you making a noise on purpose?" he asked.

After some hesitation came an answer in the affirmative: —

"Y-y-yes."

"Does not her singing please you?"

"Well, no. Why does she howl?" declared one of the boys, with vexation.

"So you wish to protest against her singing?" asked Lyeff Nikolaevitch, in a serious tone.

"Yes!"

"Then go out and say so, or stand in the middle of the room and tell every one present. That would be rude, but upright and honest. But you have got together and are squealing like grasshoppers in a corner. I will not endure such protests."

Nevertheless, the protester did not follow the advice of Lyeff Nikolaevitch, but only burst out laughing and became silent.

I afterward learned that very rarely is there an evening when there are no guests at the Tolstoys'. They tried to establish fixed days for receptions, but it ended in nothing. On the reception days the friends of Countess Sophia Andreevna chiefly assembled, and on the other days, beginning from seven o'clock in the evening, the outer door with the spring began to bang as before, and to admit various visitors to Lyeff Nikolaevitch.

And who all did not come to that little wooden house, painted a dark ocher? Learned men and writers, painters and artists, statesmen and financiers, governors, sectarians, officials of the County Council, senators, students, military men, factory laborers, peasants, correspondents of all shades and nationalities, and so forth and so on. Not a winter's day passed by without some new face making its appearance in Long-Weaver's Lane, in quest of an interview with the celebrated Russian writer.

But all his visitors may be divided into two principal categories: 1, "spectators," who present themselves to L. Tolstoy exclusively as to a celebrity, and 2, "the heavy-laden," that is, those who seek from Lyeff Nikolaevitch coöperation, advice, aid.

The "spectators," in the majority of cases, depart from L. N. Tolstoy disenchanted, and only pretend to be in ecstasies over him. In reality, he does not give them that which they seek and which he might give them. Although he is an idealist in his views, he cannot, nevertheless, endure idle conversations, and is inclined only to businesslike, practical conversations.

As he possesses a keen, penetrating mind, and wide experience of life, he frequently with one glance grasps the inward contents of the visitor, and immediately places himself upon a footing of perfect equality with him, or, as it were, freezes up himself.

It was announced to L. Tolstoy that a strange lady wished to see him. He was not at leisure, but he received her, and, in a businesslike tone, inquired what she wanted. On seeing him, his visitor became embarrassed, but mastered her emotion, and announced with decision: —

"I have read your last work, and was brought to a stop by several passages. They are incomprehensible to me."

"So that 's it!" said Lyeff Nikolaevitch, brightening up; and, inviting his visitor to his study, he spent several hours in conversation with her.

They parted friends, and, in speaking of her, he always seemed, as it were, to be illuminated from within.

One day some one said, in his presence, that she ought to be valued at her weight in gold. He corrected this:—

"No, no! She ought to be valued at her weight in the most precious stones."

Another female visitor came to him in order to place her large property at his disposal. He was touched, but declined the proposal.

"God protect us from such huge sums! One infallibly gets into trouble with them."

Lyeff Tolstoy's popularity often occasions him comical encounters, which he himself sometimes tells about afterward with inimitable comicalness. One day, in Moscow, he was walking along a narrow sidewalk, when an extremely drunken man crawled, staggering, along to meet him. When the stranger caught sight of Lyeff Nikolaevitch, he came to anchor, as it were, and with twisting tongue inquired:—

"Count Tolstoy?—Y-yes?"

"Yes."

"I am your adorer and imitator," said the fellow, with feeling, and respectfully made way for his exemplar.

On another occasion a certain citizen presented himself before Lyeff Nikolaevitch, and announced:—

"I should like *to go over to your Illustrious Highness's creed.*"

Still more amusing was the appearance of two American women. One day, Lyeff Nikolaevitch was informed that two American women wished to see him, and that they had come to Moscow for that special purpose. He received them, and entered into conversation.

The Americans announced with much aplomb that they had performed something in the nature of a feat, namely, they had made a tour of the globe, having set out from different points in America, with the agreement that they were to meet in Moscow to see "the great writer of the Russian land." And behold, they had accomplished the aim they had in view, and were content that they had carried out their mission. He smiled, and said:—

"But I think that you might have made a better use of your time."

One of the Americans exclaimed: —

"I was convinced that *Leo Tolstoy* would infallibly say something of that sort."

And, overflowing with satisfaction, the grateful visitors took their leave of L. N. Tolstoy.

As he hardly ever refuses to receive any one, Lyeff Nikolaevitch on some days is greatly fatigued by visitors, because some of them often demand an augmentation of patience and great endurance. An "admirer" arrives, and after a lyrical preface begins to demonstrate that he is in extreme need of a certain sum of money, and so extraordinarily in need that there is nothing to be done but to take it out and hand it over.

"But I have no money," declares Lyeff Nikolaevitch.

"It cannot be. You are a millionaire. Moreover, your works bring you in an income of tens of thousands. In conclusion, every line of yours is, so to speak, capital of a certain sort."

"Nevertheless, I cannot comply with your request."

"This is inhuman, Count! Then why do you preach about self-sacrifice, when you refuse me a paltry twenty-five rubles, which are absolutely necessary to me? This is the fourth month that I have been walking the streets of Moscow from morning till night, in order to get myself a ticket to Kaluga. Understand, Count, I have been walking, in vain, for *four* months."

"But in that space of time you might have walked to Kaluga several times over."

This comment dumfounded the visitor for a moment. But he promptly recovered himself, and, with complete conviction of his own uprightness, began to demonstrate that he *could not* travel on foot, like a common peasant, and eat whatever came to hand, because he was of a good family, and not in a condition to eat bad food; he must have good food.

Some visitors go even farther, and make downright threats to kill themselves if their request is not complied with.

Such visits always greatly disturb Lyeff Nikolaevitch. "You look at a visitor of that sort," said he one day, "and you feel dreadfully. You perceive that such people are precisely the ones who are *capable of anything*, except of making a moral effort over themselves. Such a spectacle is terrible!"

A painful impression is also produced upon him by visitors who present themselves to him for the purpose of enlisting him in some cause which is contrary to the principles of his soul. He experienced something of that sort in connection with the visit of the well-known French poet Déroulède, who came to Lyeff Nikolaevitch with the object of enticing him with his idea of "revenge." In the end, Lyeff Nikolaevitch, who, generally, treats foreigners with particular cordiality, could endure it no longer, and replied with vehemence to Déroulède's tirade: —

"The frontiers of kingdoms should be determined, not by the sword and blood, but by the rational agreement of nations. And when there are no longer any people who do not understand this, then there will be no more wars."

Thereupon, L. N. rose, and, in much agitation, left the room.

This scene created a sensation. Déroulède took umbrage, and when Lyeff Nikolaevitch returned, he informed him that he considered his reasoning artificial, because the first Russian peasant you might meet would certainly reason more justly; and, in proof of the justice of his cause, Déroulède proposed that his appeal should be translated into Russian for the first Russian peasant at hand. Lyeff Nikolaevitch assented. They set out for a walk. Prokofiy, a peasant of Yasnaya Polyana, met them. L. N. called him up, and translated Déroulède's pathetic harangue to the effect that the Russians and the French are brethren, but that between them stands the German, who prevents them from embracing each other, and therefore Déroulède proposed that Prokofiy should lend a hand to squeeze the fat out of the German.

Prokofiy listened attentively, reflected, and said:—

"No, Master, let it, rather, be in this way: Do you French work, and we Russians will also work, and after our toil is over, we will go to the public-house, and we will take the German with us."

This combination did not satisfy Déroulède.

CHAPTER IV

The female visitors who come to Lyeff Nikolaevitch sometimes join hysterics to their persistent demands.

One lady made her appearance and announced that she absolutely must have, in all haste, several thousand rubles, and that it was perfectly easy for adorable Lyeff Nikolaevitch to do her that favor, because he was so kind, so good, and, probably, would not take upon his soul all the results which his refusal would entail. He endeavored, in every way, to calm his visitor. But nothing would calm her except the stated sum, and not one kopek less. On being refused, the visitor uttered a shriek, and fell down in a so-called swoon. She was restored to consciousness, and offered a small sum of money for her traveling expenses. She took it, and departed with disenchanted aspect.

Ladies, in general, very frequently vanquish Lyeff Nikolaevitch, by expressing their sympathy and their wishes in such a theatrical form, as almost always induces in him a state of irritation, and then upon his features a very harsh and bristling quality makes its appearance, which reminds one of old Prince Bolkonsky, in *War and Peace*.

Some women visitors present themselves, and immediately say: —

"Lyeff Nikolaevitch, teach us life!"

Such demonstrative apparitions always put him out of countenance.

In the winter of 1896, after the first representation in the Little Theater, Moscow, of *The Power of Darkness*, a crowd of students betook themselves straight from the theater to Weaver's Lane, to L. N. Tolstoy, "in order to express to him their sentiments of gratitude and love."

The students thronged about the gates of the house

where L. N. lives, and began to hold a council, as to how they should proceed to carry out their premeditated plan. Was it timely to present themselves at such an hour, even with the object of expressing kind feelings? Lyeff Nikolaevitch might be already asleep at that moment. But Lyeff Nikolaevitch was making a call at the time, and returned home with one of his friends just as the students were discussing the matter. He was very much astonished at the unusual assemblage in Weaver's Lane, and, slipping unperceived through the ranks of the students, he entered the yard. But they instantly divined the identity of the old man who had entered the house, and they cautiously rang the bell.

"We have come to express to Lyeff Nikolaevitch our profound gratitude for *The Power of Darkness*," said the spokesman.

When he was informed of the students' request, he became extremely embarrassed.

"Why are they doing this? What shall I say to them?"

And when, a few minutes later, the throng of students entered the vestibule, and one of them, mounting a chair, in an agitated voice addressed a greeting to Lyeff Nikolaevitch, while the others darted forward to kiss his hands, he was agitated, and, for some time, could not speak.

Something similar took place also at the time of the last Congress of Naturalists in Moscow.

L. N. Tolstoy went to hear the report of his old friend, Professor Tz——. Some one present, perceiving Lyeff Nikolaevitch, ejaculated in a challenging whisper: —

"Lyeff Nikolaevitch is here!"

These words ran through the hall like lightning. Every one began to look about, to see the famous writer. Lyeff Nikolaevitch felt that one of those hypnotizing scenes which he has always avoided was beginning, and tried to slip out unperceived.

The vast throng which filled the University hall was stirred, and shouted: —

"Lyeff Nikolaevitch! Lyeff Nikolaevitch!"

Finally, the managers were obliged to request Lyeff Nikolaevitch to occupy the place of honor on the platform. The walls trembled with the applause wherewith the naturalists greeted the great Russian writer. This scene greatly disturbed L. N., and he does not like to recall it. But every simple, artless expression of sympathy touches him deeply. And if some of his visitors sometimes cause him displeasure, others, on the contrary, afford him lofty gratification, by laying bare before him whole beds of spiritual riches.

In one of his letters, Lyeff Nikolaevitch writes:—

"It is joyful to hear of influence over other people, because only then are you convinced that the fire within you is genuine when it sets aflame." And this sweetness of consciousness Lyeff Nikolaevitch sometimes extracts from his incessant association with people.

And who knows whether he could understand men's characters on all sides, and so delicately feel the pulse of mankind, without these daily encounters and conversations?

To sit out an evening at his house occasionally means to enter immediately into the current of the most vitally interesting questions, which are agitating the thoughtful part of society at the moment, and to make acquaintance with the representatives of all possible classes and tendencies.

CHAPTER V

EVENING is drawing on. The clock has struck seven, Lyeff Nikolaevitch is sitting, after dinner, in his study, with his leg tucked up under him, and listening with great interest to a young scientific man, who is telling about a new theory of light; from time to time he touches the hand of his interlocutor in a friendly manner, and makes brief remarks, which show that the question is perfectly clear to him. The servant announces the arrival of a village schoolmaster, who has come from the South. A gentleman enters, attired in Russian fashion, with sunburned face and irresolute manners. But he talks calmly, and expresses his thoughts clearly. A conversation arises concerning the situation of the school question in Russia, which Lyeff Nikolaevitch takes greatly to heart, having practical knowledge thereof, as the organizer of schools in Yasnaya Polyana.

A new visitor makes his appearance, well known for his activity in country matters. He has a whole budget of news, touching favorable enterprises in the realm of agriculture.

A spirited conversation begins about communal farming, about agricultural workmen's associations, about intelligent tillage. Lyeff Nikolaevitch feels a vivid sympathy "for the movement in the country," but considers the occupation of agriculture a very difficult problem for contemporary educated people.

"That is so plain," said he; "the peasant fixes the price of grain. That means that one must reduce one's budget and the cost of production to his rule; that is to say, one must also limit one's wants as the peasant has limited them. But is that easy for the contemporary man, who is weak and incapable of tenacious physical toil? There is the American, who, when he hires a field laborer, first of all steps up and feels the man's muscles. 'Good for nothing,' he says, and walks off. And, in truth, without firm muscles, what sort of workman is he?"

New visitors make their appearance: a Moscow financier, then a lady who lives in England.

A conversation begins with her about England, about several members of Parliament with whom she is acquainted, and about English Laborers' Associations.

A student and a scholar in the Gymnasium enter the study. The Gymnasium scholar gives Lyeff Nikolaevitch a new collection of poems by a new poetess, concerning whose writings Lyeff Nikolaevitch has heard a great deal, and has desired to make acquaintance with them.

He thanks the Gymnasium lad, opens the book, reads a few lines, and laughs.

"Listen, for heaven's sake!" he says, moving his seat closer to the light, and he reads aloud a very poetical poem.

But at the end he pauses, and in perplexity delivers the last line, which is distinguished by a pungently erotic character.

"Why was not she ashamed to print that?" asks Lyeff Nikolaevitch, in amazement; then he turns over a few leaves, again reads aloud a poem, and again it ends with an erotic aroma. Lyeff Nikolaevitch closes the book in despair, and pushes it away from him.

The conversation passes on to contemporary literature.

L. N. Tolstoy reads a very great deal, and in this respect follows the rule which Auguste Comte called *hygiene of the brain.* In addition to the Russian and foreign journals and newspapers which he receives, his friends send him everything of the slightest importance which makes its appearance in print; in consequence of which, a conversation with L. N. Tolstoy on literature always assumes the most interesting character; one learns of many novelties with which one would never have succeeded in making acquaintance to the end of one's days.

Sometimes the character of the visitors is even more varied; side by side with a magister of philosophy sits a sunburned peasant, who has come from the South and who good-naturedly addresses L. N. Tolstoy as *grandfather*.

Lyeff Nikolaevitch's unconstraint and simplicity prevent these motley assemblies from shocking any one. Here every one feels himself at home, and, at the same time, close to the others, in consequence of which L. N. Tolstoy's Moscow study presents a sort of All-Russia junction, through which have passed, during the last ten years, not a few intellectual and artistic treasures.

CHAPTER VI

ALTHOUGH L. N. Tolstoy loves friendly conversation, and friendly sociability with people, nevertheless he cherishes an almost unhealthy antipathy to everything ceremonial, populous, or crowded, in consequence of which he very rarely makes his appearance in social gatherings, and obstinately keeps away from all festivities, jubilees, and other thronged places, confining himself to attending a few public lectures which possess some special interest.

Lyeff Nikolaevitch visits the theater also very seldom, and always watches his chance to slip in unperceived, and to occupy a seat where he can be seen as little as possible.

In the winter of 1895, when he began his work on Art, he happened, for a time, to get into the theatrical zone and visited the theaters, talked with the actors, and even read his play, *The Power of Darkness*, to the artists of the Little Theater, in the theater office.

But a year later he looked upon this as a mistaken enthusiasm, and when an acquaintance began to entice Lyeff Nikolaevitch with a new opera, he said, with a smile: —

"No, no! I only kicked over the traces in that way last year, but now I have sunk to the bottom for good."

His visits to the theater did not satisfy him.

I happened to see him after a representation of *King Lear*. He was dissatisfied with the manner in which he had spent his evening, and said: —

"I gazed at those grimaces and thought: but war must be waged against all this. How much routine there is in it which overwhelms the truth. Ruskin said that Shakespeare had no villains. What nonsense! Edmund is a thorough, conventional villain."

Neither did *The Power of Darkness* satisfy him on the stage.

"In the case whence I borrowed that theme," said he, "Nikita, in a fit of delirium, kills his wife with a cart-shaft, and only then does the moral rupture take place within him. It seemed to me that that would be excessive. But my fears were vain; I ought to have introduced that scene."

"And how did the acting of it please you?" I asked.

"That was all right. Only the actors make great efforts to be natural. That should not be done. The performers ought to conceal their intentions. Generally, as soon as you perceive that they are trying to work on your feelings or to make you laugh, you immediately begin to experience the diametrically opposite sentiment. And the characters in *The Power of Darkness* are not in the least the people I thought them to be. Nikita is not a fop, he is not a dashing young sprig, but merely an offshoot of city culture. Akim does not 'discourse' when he talks; he makes great efforts, he hurries and perspires with the exertion of thought. He ought to be nervous and restless."

A little later, Lyeff Nikolaevitch again spoke about *King Lear*, and, as he felt hungry, he turned to his daughters:—

"Regan! Goneril! is your old father to have any oatmeal porridge to-day?"

Lyeff Nikolaevitch is not very enthusiastic over Shakespeare in general, and, as it seems to me, he is insufficiently acquainted with him in detail. He never quotes him and does not reënforce his speech with the winged thoughts in which Shakespeare is so rich. But, for example, Lyeff Nikolaevitch quite frequently introduces, in German, different poetical fragments from Goethe, although, at the same time, he does not belong to the latter's warm admirers, but thoroughly shares Heine's opinion, that Goethe is *a great man in a silken coat.* With Heine's works L. N. made real acquaintance only of late, and was much carried away with them.

In the midst of the most vehement conversation, he sometimes pauses and, raising his head, he recites in a masterly manner, in German, one of Heine's poems which bears upon the conversation. The poem entitled, *Lass die frommen Hypotesen*, pleases him in particular.

Lyeff Nikolaevitch has been obliged to refresh his memory of Schiller of late also. The work of Schiller which pleases him most is *The Robbers*, because of its youthful, fervent language.

"*Don Carlos* is not the same," he says. "But the principal thing which repels me in *Don Carlos* is that which I never can endure,—the exclusive nature of the situation. In my opinion, it is exactly the same as if one were to take the Siamese Twins for heroes."

Until the other day, Lyeff Nikolaevitch knew nothing whatever about Bernier, and read several of his articles with great satisfaction.

But, on the other hand, in the realm of philosophical literature he is extremely well read, and, in that direction, it is hardly probable that any of the Russian writers could be placed on a level with him.

An extraordinary thing happened with Lyeff Nikolaevitch's collection of Western writers. When he was abroad, in the '50's, he purchased the works of the prominent European authors in the original languages.

"But, alas!" he said, with a comic sigh, "they took all those books away from me on the frontier for examination, and—they are still examining them."

Among Lyeff Tolstoy's favorite thinkers and writers are: Socrates, Epictetus, Pascal, J. J. Rousseau, Victor Hugo, Dickens, and so forth. J. J. Rousseau has had more influence than all the rest on his spiritual organization.

"I deified Rousseau to such a degree," said Lyeff Nikolaevitch one day, "that, at one time, I wished to have his portrait inserted in a locket and wear it on my breast instead of a holy picture (*ikóna*)."

Nevertheless, it was not J. J. Rousseau, but Sterne, who imparted to Lyeff Nikolaevitch his first impulse to write. He once confessed as much to a Gymnasium scholar, who asked him at what age he began to write. Lyeff Nikolaevitch smiled, and said:—

"And you are afraid that you are too old? My first work was written at the age of sixteen. It was a philosophical treatise after the manner of Sterne."

CHAPTER VII

Among Russian writers, Lermontoff exercised the greatest influence on L. N. Tolstoy. To this day he cherishes a warm feeling for him, and values in him that quality which he calls *seeking*. Bereft of that quality, he considers the talent of a writer incomplete and, as it were, defective. The *rôle* of the writer, in his opinion, should include two indispensable properties: artistic talent and understanding, — that is to say, the purified side of mind, which is capable of penetrating into the actuality of phenomena and giving the loftiest view of the world of its time.

Among the Russian contemporaries of L. N. Tolstoy, D. Grigorovitch had some influence upon his literary formation. But L. N. Tolstoy is indebted for literary development and tendency more than to any one else to his elder brother, Nikolai, — a man with a brilliant, noble, and finely cultured heart.

L. N. Tolstoy has always regarded Turgeneff as a leading man, well educated and very talented; but his productions in the realm of belles-lettres, with the exception of *The Diary of a Sportsman*, never evoked rapture in L. N., and, of course, he could not nourish himself on them.

A very characteristic episode once occurred with him, which may have served, in part, to intensify the shadow which lay between Turgeneff and L. Tolstoy.

In 1860 L. Tolstoy went to visit Turgeneff in the country. The latter, just at that time, had completed his romance *Fathers and Children*, and attributed great importance to his new work, expressing a desire to learn L. N. Tolstoy's opinion of it. The latter took the manuscript, lay down with it on the divan in the study, and began to read. But the romance appeared to him so artificially constructed and so insignificant in contents that he could not overcome the weariness which seized upon him, and — he fell asleep.

"I awoke," he relates, "with a queer sort of sensation, and when I opened my eyes I beheld Turgeneff's gigantic figure retiring from the study."

All that day something seemed to be suspended between them.

But Tolstoy esteems Turgeneff very highly as the author of *The Diary of a Sportsman*, and considers his descriptions of nature as not only superb, but as unattainable by any other writer whomsoever.

L. N. Tolstoy treats Dostoevsky as an artist with profound respect, and considers some of his things — especially *Crime and Punishment* — as wonderful. But there is much in Dostoevsky that repels him. Some writers L. N. Tolstoy does not recognize at all, as it were. In this category belong Melnikoff-Petchersky, Pomyalovsky, Ryeschetnikoff, and a number of the contemporary literary workers. Among the popular writers, L. N. Tolstoy always speaks with animation of Slyeptzoff.

It is a fact not devoid of interest that L. N. Tolstoy gave to Turgeneff the idea of the little literary sketches which afterward appeared in print under the title of *Poems in Prose*. He himself tried his powers in that style of writing, but made a failure of it. He once wrote a little thing of that sort, and sent it to I. Aksakoff's journal, *Russia*, over the name of an old woman, Natalya Petrovna, who lived with the Tolstoys. But shortly afterward I. Aksakoff returned the manuscript, with a polite excuse that he could not print it because the author was, as yet, insufficiently skilled in the art of expression.

Lyeff Nikolaevitch experienced the genuine writer's fever while he was in the Caucasus, — that is to say, when he was twenty-one years of age. Dissatisfied with the idle life which he was leading in the circle of his comrades, and pining with homesickness for his native land, L. N. began to transport himself in imagination to familiar spots. This afforded him such lofty pleasure that he decided to fix some recollections on paper, and he began to jot them down. Thus *Childhood* was composed. Dreams of literary glory arose later on. As he obeyed in his creative work the imperative necessity which lay in his soul, so he drew forth from his soul that peculiar tone with which this remarkable work is permeated. He no longer places any special value on it.

Once upon a time, Lyeff Nikolaevitch was driving, with an acquaintance of his, in a public cab, in Moscow. The driver recognized him, and, turning round, said: —

"I have read a great many of your books, your Illustrious Highness! I have read *The Prisoners of the Caucasus*, I have read *Master and Workman;* I have also read about merchant Aksenoff (*God sees the truth but will not speedily reveal it*). Everything gave me great pleasure. But I have not been able, by any means, to get your book *Childhood and Boyhood*. They say it is a go-o-od book!"

L. N. Tolstoy chatted with the cabman and said to him: —

"If you are so fond of reading, come to me, and I will give you books."

"Will you give me *Childhood and Boyhood?*" asked the cabman, with animation.

"No, that is a frivolous little book. In my youth I wrote a great deal of nonsense. I will give you *Walk in the Light while there is Light.* That is far better than *Childhood and Boyhood.*"

But Lyeff Nikolaevitch's companion said to the cabman: —

"Nevertheless, do you get and read *Childhood and Boyhood.* Don't believe that it is a 'frivolous' book. It's a go-o-od little book, brother!"

Lyeff Nikolaevitch made no reply.

But, on the following day, when the cabman came to him for books, he did not give him *Childhood and Boyhood*, nevertheless, as though he did not wish to take that sin upon his soul.

But we cannot regard *Childhood and Boyhood* in that light. That work possesses, in our eyes, a double value, — both from the artistic standpoint and from the historical-literary standpoint. It gave an impetus to the genius of Lyeff Tolstoy, and, having secured for him a conspicuous success in the literary world, helped him to effect the change from the military to the literary career.

And with what sympathy, nervously straining to youthful conceit, his first steps in literature were welcomed, may be judged from the fact that, in the briefest possible time, L. Tolstoy was reckoned among the vanguard of literature; and, both in the illustrations and the caricatures of that period, he was depicted, as an equal among equals, with the most famous writers of the day: Gontcharoff, Turgeneff, Nekrasoff, Ostrovsky, and so forth.

The remarkable charm of simplicity and sincerity in *Childhood and Boyhood* captivated every one.

In his *Youth* there is a poetical chapter, in which L. N. describes how once, early in the morning, he gave himself up to the contemplation of his surroundings, and "tears, as of some unsatisfied but agitating joy," involuntarily sprang to his eyes. Once I told him of what I always thought when I read that chapter. He listened to me, and, after a considerable pause, he declared, as though recalling something, that when he wrote that chapter, he had experienced precisely those thoughts which I had mentioned. Behold the great secret of art, which knows no limits, either of time or of space.

The majority of the persons introduced in *Childhood and Boyhood*, and in *Youth*, are taken directly from life. Only, many people are mistaken when they think that the father introduced by L. N. Tolstoy in *Childhood and Boyhood* is his own father. He is Islenieff, Countess Sophia Andreevna's grandfather, a neighbor of the Tolstoys on his estate. Lyeff Nikolaevitch's grandfather, Count Ilya Andreevitch Tolstoy, was the spendthrift of his day, and squandered, in addition to his own very considerable property, the still greater property of his wife, by birth a Princess Gortchakoff. How prodigal he was may be judged from the fact that he did not have his linen washed in Russia, but sent it, by special wagons, to Holland.

His son Nikolai (the father of L. N. Tolstoy), on the contrary, was distinguished for his persistent, toilsome perseverance. When, after his father's death, he found himself without means, he assumed all his father's liabilities, and, by degrees, satisfied all the creditors, though he had on his hands various relatives, among whom was Mme. T. A. Ergoloff, who afterward reared Lyeff Nikolaevitch.

COUNT TOLSTOY DURING THE WORKING SEASON
IN THE COUNTRY

FROM A SKETCH BY L. PASTERNAK

his wife, by [illegible]
and he was [illegible]
have his [illegible]
[illegible] to Holland.

His son [illegible]
the contrary, was [illegible]
some [illegible]. When [illegible]
found himself [illegible]
[illegible], and [illegible]
though he [illegible]
whom was [illegible]
Lyeff Nikolaevitch.

CHAPTER VIII

In the family chronicles of the Counts Tolstoy, there is one very interesting episode. The father of Lyeff Nikolaevitch, in 1813, after the siege of Erfurt, was sent to St. Petersburg with despatches, and on his way back, in the hamlet of Saint Obi, he was taken prisoner together with his serf-orderly. The latter, without being observed, concealed all his master's money in his boot, and for a period of several months, during which they were imprisoned, *he never once took off his boots and foot-cloths*. His leg became chafed, and a sore was formed, but he never even showed, during all that time, that he was suffering. But, after the entry into Paris, Count Nikolai Ilitch was able to live without feeling the want of anything, and he always held the faithful orderly in kindly memory.

Thus that profound feeling which L. Tolstoy cherishes for the spiritual powers of the Russian man has in it, as it were, hereditary roots. And these roots have, gradually, descended deeper within him under the influence of acquaintance with the people, — now in the character of an active landowner and mediator of the peace, again in the character of village schoolmaster, curiously inquiring into every detail of his Yasnaya Polyana school, and again, in conclusion, through free communion with the common people during the periods of field labors and journeys on foot in company. Thanks to his attire and to his ease of manner, Lyeff Nikolaevitch everywhere succeeds in establishing free relations with the common people, and hears from them their entirely unvarnished opinions.

One day he was walking with a friend of his from Moscow to Tula. On the road, near a heap of rubbish, they saw a peasant, who was angrily breaking off the heel of his boot with a stone, and swearing vigorously. He had chafed his heel with his boot, and this had greatly enraged him. The wayfarers approached him, entered into conversation with him, and then they proceeded on their way together. The workman had a dissatisfied air, and he kept complaining of the injustice of people: he had been working in a factory, but the owner had not paid him as much as he should "for casting." Lyeff Nikolaevitch continued to listen to the workman, and then said seriously: —

"There's something wrong about that, Ivan Semyonoff!"

"May God strike me dead, if everything is not as I am telling you!" returned Ivan Semyonoff, hotly; and, in confirmation of his words, he showed Lyeff Nikolaevitch a receipt from the factory.

Thus they journeyed for about three days, halting at posting-stations for rest, and already chatting like old friends. Ivan Semyonoff inquired, with curiosity, one day when he found himself alone with Lyeff Nikolaevitch's companion: —

"Say, who is that Lyeff Nikolaevitch, if you please?"

"Oh, just an old man. Why?"

"He's a divine old man!"

At their last halting-place the travelers drank tea. Lyeff Nikolaevitch took leave of Ivan Semyonoff, and said: —

"How well it was that God led us to make acquaintance, and to pass our time together. But it still seems to me, Ivan Semyonoff, that you have not yet told us the whole truth about yourself."

Tears rose to Ivan Semyonoff's eyes.

"Forgive me, Lyeff Nikolaevitch, I told you a lie; I received all my money in full from the proprietor, and drank it up, accursed man that I am."

On another occasion, Lyeff Nikolaevitch and his traveling companion overtook on the road an ailing lad, who was very weak, and they took him with them. The mistress of the posting-station, when she saw that the lad was very ill, flew into a rage, and screamed: —

"Begone, begone! Why have you brought hither a dead man? He will die here."

Lyeff Nikolaevitch remained silent for a little while, then said gently: —

"This lad does not belong to us, he is a stranger. We took him because he was helpless. Reflect how painful it would be for you if you were in a helpless condition and no one was willing to help you."

The mistress softened, received the travelers, cared for the lad in a motherly way, and then kept repeating to him: —

"Here, you see, kind people have picked you up and brought you hither. And if there were no kind people — if there were no kind people in the world, what would happen then?"

Free and frequent intercourse with the common people has enabled Lyeff Nikolaevitch to accumulate a great hoard of knowledge concerning the life of the people, and to perfect that rich, highly colored language which renders him a master in the most varied realms of thought and feeling.

In conversation with the peasants Lyeff Nikolaevitch never apes their tone, but bears himself simply and seriously, like an experienced, clever peasant, who knows all the shades of peasant life. He knows what to say and to whom, and how to get hold of each one.

In the course of one of his journeys, he entered a village posting-station to spend the night. The master of the station, a stubborn, capricious old man, flew into a rage with his young son over something or other, and began to beat him, then seized him by the hair, and dragged him from the room. Lyeff Nikolaevitch began to reason with the peasant. But the latter got angry and paid no attention to him. Then Lyeff Nikolaevitch said to him reproachfully: —

"Shame on you! Why, even a wild beast would not do that to another wild beast. And you call yourself a Christian. Aren't you afraid that God will punish you?"

This stung the peasant, and he shouted wrathfully: —

"So, according to your wise head, a man must not teach his children?"

"He must teach, but not *beat* them," said Lyeff Nikolaevitch.

"And do you know what Count Aratchkeeff said?" inquired the peasant, in a malicious, challenging voice.

"What?"

"*Kill nine men, but teach the tenth* —"

Before the peasant could finish his sentence, Lyeff Nikolaevitch sprang at him with flaming eyes, and shouted: —

"Don't you dare to talk like that! God is not in you. And you must know, the man who said that was a wild beast."

And, as he said this, there was something in his face and voice before which the rage of the harsh peasant was instantly extinguished.

The piercing keenness of the glance with which Lyeff Nikolaevitch sometimes seems to bore through a man and to reach the very depths of his soul, often renders a lie impossible to the people with whom he is talking.

A tragic event occurred at Yasnaya Polyana in 1896: the coachman found a dead baby in the pond. The whole Tolstoy family was greatly upset at this occurrence. One of Lyeff Nikolaevitch's daughters was overwhelmed, in particular, because she was almost convinced that the dead baby belonged to a cross-eyed widow, who had concealed her pregnancy. But the widow obstinately spurned the accusation brought against her, and swore that she was innocent.

Suspicions against other people began to circulate.

Before dinner, Lyeff Nikolaevitch betook himself to the park, in order to have a little stroll, but soon returned with a weary and agitated mien. He had been in the village, to the cross-eyed widow's. He did not argue with her at all, but merely listened attentively to what she had to say, and then remarked: —

"If this murder is not the work of your hands, then it will cause you no suffering. But if you committed it, you must feel very sad now; so sad that nothing else in this life can ever seem painful to you."

"Oh, what a weight I have upon my heart now, as though some one were crushing it with a stone!" cried the widow, breaking into sobs, and she frankly confessed to Lyeff Nikolaevitch that she had strangled her baby, and thrown it into the water. That is why he was so melancholy.

CHAPTER IX

FAMILIARITY with the life of the Russian people could not pass over such a sensitive nature as that of L. N. Tolstoy without leaving traces. With his powerfully developed sense of human dignity, he could not but suffer painfully, when he beheld around him crying want and ignorance. And Lyeff Nikolaevitch was seized by the desire to alleviate, if only in a small degree, the lot of his common people. He began to take their interests more and more to heart, and, at last, he went over to popular literature for the people. He visited the night lodging-houses, compiled almanacs for the people, primers and little books wlth popular expositions concerning the air, the work of the sun, and so forth, and so forth.

This was not a sudden leap to one side, but a deliberate turn into a path which he had previously overlooked.

To use his own words, he reminded one of a man who, after having chosen a familiar path, turns back. Everything which had been on his left hand is now on his right, and everything which had been on his right hand is now on his left.

Though enthusiastically engrossed in 1891, by a work which was of very great importance to him, L. N. Tolstoy, nevertheless, without hesitation, cast it aside, cast aside his rooted habits, which are not easily discarded at his age, and went off for several months to the famine district, in order to alleviate the lot of the starving.

By his own personal exertions, Lyeff Nikolaevitch founded more than two hundred soup-kitchens, traveling to and fro, over the snow-drifts, from village to village, through snow-storms and snapping cold.

Not a little labor, requiring discretion, tact, energy, and

patience, was involved in the establishment of each of these soup-kitchens. It was necessary to keep complicated accounts concerning the organization, the receipt of contributions, the assignment of provisions, the procuring and despatch of various materials.

L. N. Tolstoy's appeal received responses from every direction, even from abroad. Every one believed that they were committing their contributions to trustworthy hands. And that was a wonderful time so far as the stirring up of feelings was concerned, and still awaits its historian. Yet, nevertheless, it was but a drop in the ocean of the people's need. It became necessary to refuse, it became necessary to *make a choice among the starving*.

L. N. Tolstoy, with his inherent energy, introduced many practical novelties into the enterprise which he organized, inspiring every one with his presence. But, in spite of all his case-hardened endurance, he sometimes reached such a state of fatigue that he could not, without an effort, express at once the simplest thought; he could not, on the spur of the moment, put a name to the thing he wanted.

"Tanya," he said to his eldest daughter, who accompanied him and shared with him all the hardships of their new life, "to-morrow, without fail, we must send — "

And Lyeff Nikolaevitch, in spite of his unusually retentive memory, had forgotten what must be sent and whither it must be sent.

CHAPTER X

L. N. Tolstoy's love for the common people began to usurp, and still usurps, a considerable portion of his strength and time. He has contracted many relations in that connection which it is no longer possible to break. It is impossible to refuse to see a peasant, to get rid of him with a gift, when he asks to have a petition to the court written for him. It is impossible to put off a woman with alms, when her husband dies and the grain is not harvested. So L. N. Tolstoy writes the petition for the peasant man, and aids the mourning peasant woman to harvest the grain in the working season, patiently enduring in the process the grievous pain in his leg caused by an injury from a cart-wheel, as the orderly endured with patience the no less grievous pain for the love of his fellow-man.

But the pain from the contusion keeps increasing. Countess Sophia Andreevna goes to Moscow, and, without Lyeff Nikolaevitch's knowledge, brings back a physician, who declares that if one day more had been allowed to elapse, a catastrophe would have ensued. Lyeff Nikolaevitch's temperature has already risen to 40° (Réau.). He was obliged to go to bed, and remain there for several weeks, which gave the world *The Power of Darkness.*

The greater part of that piece was dictated by Lyeff Nikolaevitch, and occupied several weeks. None of his works came so easily to him, because he had already prepared himself for his task by laboring in the fields, and chatting with the peasants.

And to demand that he shall occupy himself exclusively with polite literature is equivalent to demanding from him the renunciation of his personality and the needs of his soul.

And it is incomprehensible how so sensitive and cultivated a man as Turgeneff failed to understand that inward fermentation which L. N. Tolstoy was passing through, and could seriously think that the author of *War and Peace* could cease to live with the artistic images, whose production constitutes for the true artist as unconquerable a necessity as is blossoming for a plant.

And Lyeff Tolstoy has never subdued in himself the author, and has not withered up that spiritual condition which is called inspiration. On the contrary, under all conditions, the thirst for creation has always, as it were, smoldered within him. And the only one of the Russian men of action with whom he can be compared, so far as this unquenchable thirst is concerned, is Anton Rubinstein.

While returning home one night last year, in Moscow, with one of his friends, Lyeff Nikolaevitch suddenly came to a halt, and, inhaling the air with avidity, he exclaimed passionately: —

"Heavens, how I want to write! My brain is seething with images."

"Then why this delay, Lyeff Nikolaevitch?" inquired his companion.

"Time is lacking. I have work for a hundred years, and I have but three days to live."

"What do you mean, Lyeff Nikolaevitch?"

"Well, a few months longer. In any case, not long. And in these remaining days I want to say something fine. Perhaps God will graciously permit me not to live out my allotted time in vain, but to do something worthy toward the end of my days. And there is so much to write about! They say that all the interesting themes are exhausted. That is not true. Here, for instance — "

And he began to unfold a theme which dealt with one side of family relations, with which, as a matter of fact, no one has as yet dealt in literature.

"There is still another subject which greatly interests me," continued Lyeff Nikolaevitch with animation: "it is the intimate union of various spiritual qualities in one and the same man. The man, who is, in reality, very clever, keen, and noble, is at the same time very narrow, petty, and insignificant. There is another interesting subject, which concerns the characters of the mind. As the characters of the passions are, so are also the characters of the mind. One man has a very vast mind, but he sees things only under a certain aspect. And things which are easily comprehensible for a smaller mind are unattainable for him. Hence proceed the various sharp conflicts in social life."

Lyeff Nikolaevitch's companion inquired:—

"Have you begun to work out any one of these themes?"

"No, everything, so far, is merely a project. I am occupied with other work at present."

A few days after this conversation, a lady inquired:—

"Is it true, Lyeff Nikolaevitch, that you are engaged in writing a novel of Caucasian life, in which one of Schamyl's companions in arms figures?"

"Yes, yes, I am writing. I am writing everything," replied Lyeff Nikolaevitch, hastily and reluctantly. Then he added, in an explanatory tone: "I say seriously that I am writing everything. You ask: Am I writing any sort of a story? I am. Am not I writing a romance? I am writing a romance also. And am not I thinking of writing a play? I am also writing a play. I am writing everything."

And, in reality, he is always writing, and writing a great deal.

But he is very far from committing to print everything he writes. He is very exacting toward himself.

In 1896 L. N. Tolstoy completed a novel over which he had labored long. Those who had heard extracts from this novel thought that, in the force of his description, our famous writer had taken another step in advance, and were convinced that, within a short time, the novel would appear in print. But he was in no haste to publish his new work, as he intended to labor a little more upon it.

But when he was questioned, lately, about the belated novel, he shook his head, and said, in the tone which people use in speaking of things which possess no interest for them: —

"No, no, I am done with that! The theme is not mine, and the manner is of the routine sort which I must abandon."

Lyeff Nikolaevitch, like the majority of writers, bears himself with some eagerness toward literary themes. When he hears a characteristic story, he immediately tries it on, as it were, and admires it all round, like a good carpenter inspecting good, dry timber. He once told us about an interesting law-case, which took place in the Moscow court-room. When he had finished his story, L. N. remarked: —

"You see, there's a regular Maupassant story, ready-made to hand. It is a genuine godsend for some young writer. However, perhaps I shall use it myself," he added hastily, as though afraid that some one would appropriate the interesting subject. Some time later, I happened to hear that he had again narrated the same episode, and I was struck by several artistic details, which had already crept into it during the interval, from the artistic laboratory of Lyeff Nikolaevitch, possibly against his will.

But a great deal is required before any theme becomes an object of his creative powers. First of all it must be distinguished by novelty, clearness, and inward worth. Then, the side of life embraced must be well known to Lyeff Nikolaevitch; he does not like to write by "hearsay." In conclusion, as a final condition, it is indispensable that the subject shall *take possession of him*, as a cough takes possession of a man. Then only can he set to work, and yield himself up to it with the enthusiasm of the true artist.

"What a splendid hunt we had to-day after that gray hare!" he said, with animation, to his wife, emerging from his study after work, and with an aspect as though he really had been engaged in a successful hunt after a gray hare. (The hunter's pulse still beats in L. Tolstoy, but he suppresses the inclination in himself, because of artistic demands.)

In his manner of working, Lyeff Nikolaevitch reminds one of the old painters. Having settled upon the plan of the work, and collected a great number of studies, he first makes a charcoal sketch, as it were, and writes rapidly, without thinking of particulars. He gives what he has thus written, to have a clean copy made, to Countess Sophia Andreevna, or to one of his daughters, or to some one of his friends to whom this work will afford pleasure.

Lyeff Nikolaevitch usually writes on quarto sheets of plain paper, of an inferior quality, in a large, involved hand, and sometimes covers as many as twenty pages in one day, which makes more than half a sheet of printed matter. But he forms no fixed habits either in regard to paper or pens, and when one of the commercial firms hit upon the idea of launching upon the world the *Tolstoy pen*, it appeared that Lyeff Nikolaevitch had no opinion on that matter. He works chiefly in the morning, between nine o'clock and three, because he regards that interval as the very best for work. It is almost impossible to get an interview with him at that time, if Countess Sophia Andreevna is at home. She carefully guards his working hours, and one may say, without sinning, that she would even refuse to admit a king to Lyeff Nikolaevitch, if the king would interfere with his work. In this respect, it is not likely that any other Russian author has had so faithful a body-guard as has Lyeff Nikolaevitch in the person of his anxious wife.

But they differ in their views of the world. He represents, as it were, heaven in his family, and she represents the earth.

But they live together on loving terms. She cares for him like an indefatigable nurse, makes his clothes with her own hands, and only parts from him for the briefest possible time. He bears himself in a Christian spirit toward her weaknesses, and highly prizes her sincerity and frankness.

CHAPTER XI

In February, 1895, the Tolstoys' youngest son died, seven-year-old Vanetchka (Johnny), a very charming little boy, who, in some degree, resembled his father in his outward appearance. Lyeff Nikolaevitch bore himself toward this painful blow with Christian resignation. Several of his acquaintances who talked with him during those sad days did not even learn of his loss. But Sophia Andreevna was stupefied with her grief, and bore it with difficulty. Life lost its interest for her, and she prayed God for death. During this sharp crisis, Lyeff Nikolaevitch treated her with that peculiar compassion and delicacy of heart which are so captivating in him. Once, it even seemed to me that he was not sincere, for the sake of not paining Sophia Andreevna. This is the way it was.

When spring approaches, Lyeff Nikolaevitch generally makes all haste to leave the city for Yasnaya Polyana. He does not like the city, and in the springtime he feels an unconquerable loathing for it. But in the spring of 1895 he remained until June in Moscow, for the sake of his grief-stricken wife, who did not wish to depart for the country until the boys had finished their examinations. At the end of May, I happened to call upon Lyeff Nikolaevitch. He looked worn out. As I was aware that he loves the country in spring, I said:—

"I think you are exhausted here."

At that moment Sophia Andreevna entered the room.

"Not in the least. I feel capitally here," exclaimed Lyeff Nikolaevitch, quickly and loudly.

She cast a grateful glance at him, and said:—

"I do not know how you feel. But it grieves me deeply that you should be living so late in Moscow for my sake in this heat and turmoil."

"You are fretting yourself for nothing. I feel very well here."

But perhaps he really did feel very well at that moment.

When the French writer Richet was visiting the Tolstoys, he is said to have remarked to Sophia Andreevna that she could not possibly have found time for personal happiness by the side of so great a husband. But it seems to me that that is a mere phrase. Within the narrow limits of human happiness, Lyeff Nikolaevitch and Sophia Andreevna have been happy in their day, and have got out of life, if not all that they might have got, at any rate, a very great deal. He has given her a clever, healthy, faithful, and passionately loving husband. She, in the very prime of his powers, gave him a quiet happiness, untroubled by storms, with a long series of domestic joys, which were afterward reflected in his works. And the future historian of Russian literature can hardly pass over Countess Sophia Andreevna without mention.

Count Sollogub, during one of his visits to Yasnaya Polyana, once said to Lyeff Nikolaevitch: —

"What a lucky man you are, my dear fellow! Fate has given you everything that one could even dream: a splendid family, a charming, loving wife, universal fame, health — everything."

"But that is not because Fate is particularly partial to me," replied Lyeff Nikolaevitch, "but because I have always wished only for that which God has sent me. He has given me that sort of a wife, and I am satisfied with her, and want no other."

In consequence of Countess Sophia Andreevna having minutely studied her husband's habits for a period of many years, she knows as soon as Lyeff Nikolaevitch emerges from his cabinet, by his very aspect, how his work has thriven, in what frame of mind he is. And if it is necessary to copy anything for him, she immediately lays aside all her own affairs, of which her hands are always full; and no matter what happens that day, at a certain hour, she will, without fail, have copied legibly all that is needed, and laid it on his writing-table.

CHAPTER XII

After his morning labors Lyeff Nikolaevitch generally goes out into the air, and if he is in Moscow, he betakes himself on foot into the city and visits his friends, or rides on horseback, or on his bicycle, according to the state of the weather. Muscular exercise in the open air is, for him, a necessity, whose place nothing else can take, but the satisfaction of which is, sometimes, allied with some risk, and causes Sophia Andreevna many anxious moments. Lyeff Nikolaevitch has gone off on horseback, or on his bicycle, and has promised to return at a certain time. Sophia Andreevna begins to get uneasy, and gloomy thoughts assail her: "At Lyeff Nikolaevitch's age, it is so easy to fall from his bicycle or from a skittish horse, and receive fatal injuries. At his time of life, he should not undertake such excursions, because his muscles have already become like a threadbare fabric. But what is one to do with him? Is it possible to dissuade him from anything?"

Her hearers, in part, share Sophia Andreevna's views, and gradually become infected with alarm.

But Lyeff Nikolaevitch enters, as usual, with fresh animation after his trip, and the clouds instantly vanish.

Once, something in the nature of a conspiracy was concocted against Lyeff Nikolaevitch's riding a bicycle. A woman doctor was visiting the Tolstoys, and thought that it was very hazardous for Lyeff Nikolaevitch to ride thirty versts on his wheel. It so happened that, on that very day, an English illustrated journal had arrived which contained an article about the injurious effects of bicycle riding.

It was decided that I, as though by accident, should begin a conversation on bicycle riding; the woman doctor was to back me up, and state her views concerning the wheel, and reënforce them by quotations from the English journal, which was to be lying open there, for greater persuasiveness. We had planned everything very craftily, and Lyeff Nikolaevitch was immediately to tumble into the nets spread for him. But our plot, like the majority of plots, broke down; and, principally, through my fault. At the most critical moment, when I ought to have made my sort of "start," I felt ashamed, as though I were about to make a fool of the man whom I deeply respect and love, and I maintained an obstinate silence, paying no heed to the signals. Then the woman doctor entered, single-handed, upon the execution of the plot. Lyeff Nikolaevitch listened to her attentively, and entirely agreed with her, that it was not right to abuse bicycle riding; then, probably suspecting in what direction the "last deductions of experimental science" pointed, he said that, twenty years previously, Professor Zakharin had strictly forbidden him all physical exercise, under penalty of its resulting badly for him.

"But," added Lyeff Nikolaevitch, "the result would certainly have been bad for me long ago, if I had obeyed Zakharin, and stopped giving my muscles the work which strengthens me, gives me sound sleep, a spirited frame of mind, and has made me like the horse out at grass. Only let the horse rest, and feed him, and he is fit for work again."

And, as though in confirmation of the justice of his views, Lyeff Nikolaevitch, with a brisk, youthful step, went off to his study, where he always has on hand some unfinished work which must be completed in haste.

CHAPTER XIII

WHEN Lyeff Nikolaevitch's new work, cleanly copied out, makes its appearance on his work-table, it is subjected to instant remodeling. But again, it is still in the nature of a charcoal sketch. The manuscript is speedily spotted all over with erasures and interpolations between the lines, at the sides, and at the bottom, and with transfers to other pages. Whole sentences are replaced by others, which, like flashes of lightning, sometimes illuminate the image presented from a new point of view. The work, cleanly copied out for the second time, suffers the same fate. The same thing happens with the third. Some chapters Lyeff Nikolaevitch writes over *more than half a score of times*. Meanwhile, he hardly troubles himself at all about the external workmanship, and even entertains a sort of repugnance to everything very finely finished in art.

"Often, all that that results in is, that it dries up thought, and injures the impression," he says.

And, arming himself more and more, as he writes, with his recollections and with new information concerning the question with which he is dealing, Lyeff Nikolaevitch toils doggedly, searchingly, and persistently over every chapter, taking only brief breaks for rest, and, generally, resorting to the laying out of a suit at Patience in moments of perplexity.

His intense seeking after inward clearness in every hero whom he depicts constitutes, at that time, Lyeff Nikolaevitch's chief anxiety, and he is fond of saying in this connection, that *gold is obtained by strenuous sifting and washing*.

Lyeff Nikolaevitch succeeds in dashing off only very few scenes at the first effort, under the influence of vivid impressions. In that manner was written the descrip-

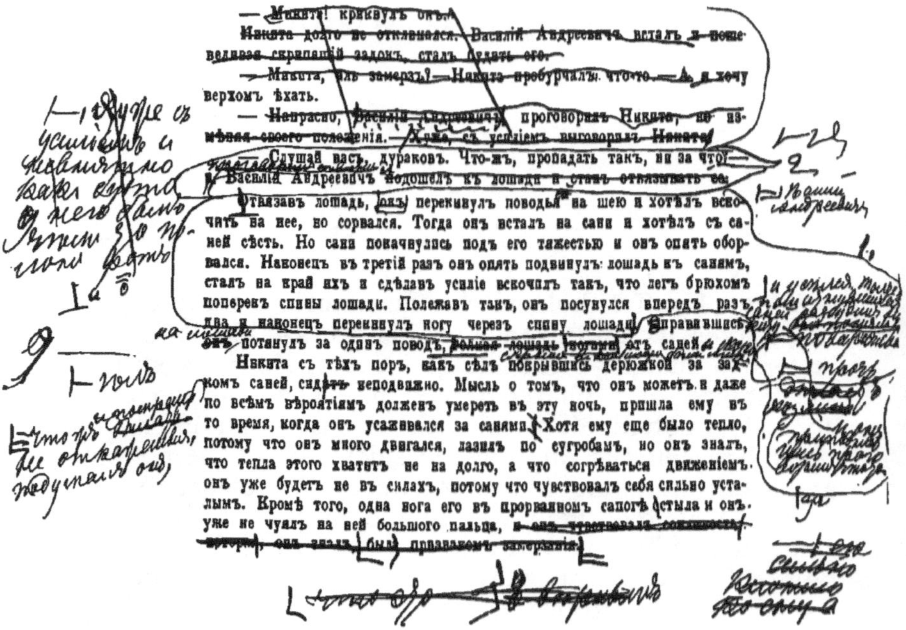

— Микита! крикнулъ онъ.

Никита долго не откликался. Василій Андреевичъ всталъ и, пошевеливая скрипавшій задокъ, сталъ будить его.

— Микита, али замерзъ? — Никита пробурчалъ что-то. — А я хочу верхомъ ѣхать.

— Напрасно, Василій Андреевичъ, проговорилъ Никита, не измѣняя своего положенія. Хуже, съ усиліемъ выговорилъ Никита.

— Слушай васъ, дураковъ. Что-жъ, пропадать такъ, ни за что?

Василій Андреевичъ подошелъ къ лошади и сталъ отвязывать ее.

Отвязавъ лошадь, онъ перекинулъ поводья на шею и хотѣлъ вскочить на нее, но сорвался. Тогда онъ всталъ на сани и хотѣлъ съ саней сѣсть. Но сани покачнулись подъ его тяжестью и онъ опять оборвался. Наконецъ въ третій разъ онъ опять подвинулъ лошадь къ санямъ, сталъ на край ихъ и сдѣлавъ усиліе вскочилъ такъ, что легъ брюхомъ поперекъ спины лошади. Полежавъ такъ, онъ посунулся впередъ разъ, два и наконецъ перекинулъ ногу черезъ спину лошади. Оправившись онъ потянулъ за одинъ поводъ, больше лошадь ногами отъ саней.

Никита съ тѣхъ поръ, какъ сѣлъ покрывшись дерюжкой за задкомъ саней, сидѣлъ неподвижно. Мысль о томъ, что онъ можетъ и даже по всѣмъ вѣроятіямъ долженъ умереть въ эту ночь, пришла ему въ то время, когда онъ усаживался за санями. Хотя ему еще было тепло, потому что онъ много двигался, лазилъ по сугробамъ, но онъ зналъ, что тепла этого хватитъ не на долго, а что согрѣваться движеніемъ онъ уже будетъ не въ силахъ, потому что чувствовалъ себя сильно усталымъ. Кромѣ того, одна нога его въ прорванномъ сапогѣ остыла и онъ уже не чуялъ на ней большого пальца, и онъ чувствовалъ сонливость, которая, онъ зналъ, была признакомъ замерзанія.

Facsimile of corrected proof from "Master and Man"

tion of the horse-race in *Anna Karenina*, under the influence of Prince Obolensky's captivating narration.

As the rewriting and correction proceed, some details stand forth more clearly, but others seem to withdraw farther and farther into the background.

When, by dint of intense labor, Lyeff Nikolaevitch has obtained a certain degree of lucidity, he reads his new work aloud in a circle of people intimately connected with him, in order that he may profit by their comments, before the book has appeared in print. When he had completed *The Power of Darkness*, he read his drama to the peasants, but derived very few instructive hints from that reading. In the most touching parts of the drama, which Lyeff Nikolaevitch cannot read without tears, several of his hearers suddenly began to laugh, and chilled the reader.

The severest critic of L. N. Tolstoy's new works is, generally, Countess Sophia Andreevna, who expresses her opinion with her characteristic straightforwardness. Lyeff Nikolaevitch sometimes agrees with her, but sometimes stoutly defends the position which he has taken up.

The long-postponed novel, previously mentioned, was rejected by Sophia Andreevna. One day, as we were drinking tea, the conversation turned on Lyeff Nikolaevitch's writings. That day Sophia Andreevna had the proofs of *War and Peace* for a new edition, and wore a rather weary air. One of the guests inquired whether reading the proofs of *War and Peace* gave her pleasure or not.

"Some passages, yes," said she; "but some did not please me formerly, and do not please me now."

"Which, for instance?"

"Just to-day I read the proofs where Pierre Bezukhoff, when taken prisoner, begins to laugh. That is forced. One cannot laugh at such a moment."

At that instant, Lyeff Nikolaevitch approached the tea-table and asked what we were talking about. Sophia Andreevna repeated her accusation, with precision.

"Why do you assert positively," he inquired, "that

it is impossible to laugh at such moments? Why, to-day, I was reading in the *Archives*, about the Decembrist Batenkoff, who, when he was put in prison, burst into a loud laugh, and said: 'You are locking me up because of my ideas. But my ideas are not here — they are roaming about in freedom.' Pierre might have laughed in exactly the same way."

"No, that is false. At such a moment it is *impossible* to laugh. And I do not understand how you can assert such a thing."

"And I do not understand how you can fail to comprehend that it is impossible to reject so stubbornly that which you do not understand."

"That is my opinion."

Lyeff Nikolaevitch put an end to the dispute, and after the lapse of a few minutes he had imperceptibly banished the little clouds which had gathered in the air.

After every altercation, and, especially, after every injustice done to him, a strong reaction begins within him, and he passes into that charming, serene frame of mind of which I have already spoken. It is opportune to mention here, that after the well-known quarrel between Turgeneff and L. N. Tolstoy at Fet-Schenschin's, — the quarrel which raised the question of a duel, and concerning which Turgeneff himself afterward said that he behaved *like a naughty little boy*, — Lyeff Nikolaevitch, of his own initiative, wrote to Turgeneff, under the influence of a kindly impulse, a conciliatory letter. But the letter was not transmitted to Turgeneff, and their strained relations continued for some time longer.

CHAPTER XIV

As soon as the rumor gets into circulation that Lyeff Tolstoy has finished a new work, men and women amateurs begin to swoop down upon him from all quarters, with requests that he will put his new book at their disposal, because of the particular circumstances in which they find themselves placed. And he generally does give his new book to some one.

But his labors over his new work do not end here. There is still the proof-reading, which usually calls forth in L. N. Tolstoy a flood of intensified activity. During the period of time while the manuscript has been in the press, so many events have occurred, so many fresh observations have accumulated which illuminate some sides of the question dealt with from an entirely new point of view. But the margins of the proof-sheets are so narrow, the time for correction is so short, and restraining the pressure of new thoughts, economizing every possible scrap of paper, Lyeff Nikolaevitch converts the proof-sheets into a closely woven net of corrections. The same thing happens to the second proofs. And it may be said, without exaggeration, that if Lyeff Nikolaevitch were to have ninety-nine sets of proofs for any one of his works, the ninety-ninth proof would be speckled with corrections.

The sense of self-criticism is strongly developed in him, and he always perceives his mistakes clearly on the following day. But in the proof-sheets his mental sharp-sightedness is still further sharpened, and some of the chapters come out altered beyond recognition.

One day, when the subject of the conversation was intense toil over mental productions, Lyeff Nikolaevitch said: —

"No trifle must be neglected in art, because, sometimes, some half-torn-off button may illuminate a certain side of the life of a given person. And the button must be depicted without fail. But all the efforts, and the half-torn-off button, must be directed exclusively to the inward substance of the matter, and must not divert the attention from the principal and important part to particulars and trifles, as so often happens. One of the contemporary writers, in narrating the history of Joseph and the wife of Potiphar, would assuredly not miss the opportunity to shine by his knowledge of life, and would write: 'Come to me, said Potiphar's wife, languidly, stretching out toward Joseph her hand delicate with the perfumed massage, with such and such a bracelet, and so forth.' And all these details not only would not illuminate the substance of the matter more clearly, but would infallibly extinguish it."

One of L. N. Tolstoy's acquaintances compares his work with viands prepared by certain thrifty housewives, who pay little heed to the outward attractiveness of the food, but concentrate their attention chiefly upon seeing that the provisions are fresh, and cleanly cooked, and that the food excels in its nutritive qualities.

And, in fact, Lyeff Nikolaevitch troubles himself very little about the outward attractiveness of his works, often heaping up one incidental proposition upon another, fitting them out with repetitions of one and the same word, and absolutely disregarding various academical rules concerning style. But, on the other hand, when it is a question of "freshness" and "purity," there is no end to his exacting demands.

I once happened to discover to what lengths his exactingness goes. The conversation, somehow, turned upon the Molokani [1] who, as is well known, do not recognize any books except those of a religious character. We were talking in particular about this, and one of those present severely condemned the one-sidedness of the Molokani. Lyeff Nikolaevitch was in one of those mental states which come upon people only after great internal changes and important conquests over self. A

[1] A religious sect — the *milk-drinkers*, literally. — Tr.

man in that state of mind seems already to have passed over the threshold of life, and to have placed himself above many human weaknesses. Communion with people who are in that condition affords such lofty delight, that there is nothing which can be compared with it. Their thoughts are penetrating, their feelings are profound and lucid. The most commonplace words acquire in their mouths remarkable force. The most gloomy situations acquire clearness and relief.

Such moments of mental illumination always seem to transfigure Lyeff Nikolaevitch's exterior. His harsh features beam, and take on a reflection of spiritual beauty. He becomes gracious, benevolent, listens patiently, speaks in a calm, friendly manner, with head slightly bowed and hands clasped. In the midst of the conversation, when his interlocutor is at a loss to express any thought, he gently lays his hand on the other's shoulder, or on his knee, and by this movement alone creates around him the atmosphere of intimacy.

Any one who has seen him at such moments forgives him for all the asperities of his character, and becomes permeated with the most profound feeling toward him that one man can entertain for another man.

Every remark of L. N. Tolstoy's at such moments acquires special value, because he reveals himself wholly, as it were, in his spiritual blossoming.

Lyeff Nikolaevitch listened attentively to his companion, who disproved of the Molokani, because they avoid worldly books, and then said thoughtfully: —

"But ought we to condemn them for that? When you sometimes reflect how many lies are piled up in our books, you find it difficult to say where there is most of it, in life or in books. And you sometimes take your pen, and write something after this fashion: 'Early in the morning Ivan Nikititch rose from his bed, and called his son to him.' And all at once you feel ashamed of yourself, and you throw down your pen. Why lie, old man? For that *did not occur*, and you know no Ivan Nikititch. Then why, in your old age, shall you have recourse to lies? Write about what has happened, what you have actually seen and lived through. No lies are needed. There are so many of them."

With such esthetic demands, of course it is impossible to write a romance every year. Even if Lyeff Nikolaevitch wished to do that now he could not, in all probability, because he has become so thoroughly imbued with the habit of endeavoring to obtain a certain lucidity of subject that he sometimes even writes his letters over several times, and meditates upon them with concentrated attention, and writes them with as much feeling as that with which a bridegroom goes forth to his wedding.

On another occasion I happened to hear Lyeff Nikolaevitch's opinion concerning his works, during a stroll in the fields. He retarded his steps for a minute, and said, with a tinge of bitterness: —

"You write, and write all sorts of novels and tales, and when you look at the life of our educated class, and compare it with the toilsome life of the common people, you are seized with shame that you are busying yourself with such trifles as writing for the educated class, and you long to renounce it all for good."

I tried to reply: —

"But how can we renounce that which has been given to us by God, in the quality of His loftiest gift? And is it possible that it is not worth our while to work for the educated class? A conviction has arisen that it was not the Prussian army, but the German scientist, who conquered France. And therein lies a certain amount of truth. Without enlightenment there cannot be that full understanding which alone can give to a man power and firmness. And so long as our people are uneducated *the Power of Darkness* will long hang over them, with all its monstrous attributes. But who, if not the educated class, can introduce enlightened principles among the masses of the common people? And do not you, by aiding the growth of education through your works, serve the common people also, simultaneously? You certainly do serve them. Therefore do not turn away from us as from unworthy persons, with your divine gift, and do not deprive us of the fine specimens of your creative power."

We were walking briskly, in consequence of which I breathed brokenly, and my speech assumed a passionate tone. Lyeff Nikolaevitch made no reply, and for some time we proceeded in silence. Then began a conversation on the problems of art. He was then meditating upon his book, *What is Art?* This work had been projected by him in the '70's, at the request of a St. Petersburg journalist. But when he then set about the work, Lyeff Nikolaevitch perceived that many fundamental questions of art were not, as yet, sufficiently fixed in his mind. And only after the lapse of seventeen years, when everything had thoroughly fermented in his mind, and had quieted down, did he at last take up the work already begun. His writing-table and shelves were loaded with piles of all possible sorts of folios, which treated of art in Russian and foreign languages.

Thanks to his numerous friends and admirers, he was able to acquaint himself with very rare and precious publications, unattainable for most people, and, in the course of several months of preparation, he seemed to live exclusively in his new work, gladly discussing it, and developing in conversation the theses he had in view. This work cost him about two years of assiduous labor.

CHAPTER XV

After the appearance of his article upon art, printed, in an abbreviated form, in the Moscow journal, *Questions of Philosophy and Psychology*, Lyeff Nikolaevitch received a number of sympathetic letters, from persons whose opinions he could not but value in the matter of art.

Thus the well-known critic, V. Stasoff, wrote to him that, although he disagreed with him on several points in his new work, he, nevertheless, considered it a notable work which presented the last word of the nineteenth century, of that great century which could end in such unprecedented truth, unknown throughout the course of many ages.

The artist Ilya Ryépin wrote to L. N. Tolstoy under the vivid impression of the newly read article: —

"Adored Lyeff Nikolaevitch! I have just read *What is Art?* and am still under the influence of the powerful impression of this mighty work of yours. If it is possible not to agree with some particulars and examples, on the other hand, the book as a whole and the presentation of questions are so profound and indisputable, that one becomes cheerful and is permeated with joy. Religion has been discovered — that is the greatest deed of your life. And I can say without hypocrisy, I am happy in having lived until this day."

All these expressions of sympathy touched Lyeff Nikolaevitch. Yet he bears himself with good-will toward the critics who do not agree with his principal propositions, but who, nevertheless, introduce his work to their readers. And only when a criticism was deliberately hostile or too vehement did he, without comment, lead the conversation to another theme. But one day, after reading a criticism of that sort, written with particular irritation, he burst out laughing, and said: —

"When you read about yourself, you, nevertheless, prize sympathy and are chagrined at blame. But in this special case, the article has given me pleasure. You feel as though you had tumbled right into the middle of an ant-heap, and they were angrily swarming about."

What Lyeff Nikolaevitch cannot endure is unmeasured praise addressed to him, and, in general, all sorts of exaggeration in the expression of feeling. This always embarrasses him, and he then becomes curt and disagreeable. In general he does not like any expressions of approbation which have the odor of incense. In such cases his pride seems to rebel because an effort is being made to capture him, not with the language of the soul, but with the honey of the tongue. One of his visitors began one day to tell him about some remarkable revival, called forth by the appearance in print of *Master and Workman*.

L. N. Tolstoy frowned, and applying to himself the words of Phocion, he interrupted the speaker: —

"Have I then written something very stupid?"

As he is very exacting toward his own works, and regards art as the most powerful of all means in the matter of disseminating good sentiments among people, L. N. Tolstoy will not tolerate any carelessness in art, and will sooner pardon lack of talent than lack of serious bearing toward any matter. And one instance of gross carelessness in the works of any person is enough to make Lyeff Nikolaevitch forever turn his back upon that author.

The conversation fell one day upon Melnikoff-Petchersky, to whom L. N. Tolstoy bore himself negatively. I inquired: —

"Lyeff Nikolaevitch, why are you so indifferent toward Melnikoff-Petchersky? He has written some very good things."

"Perhaps," said Lyeff Nikolaevitch with a suggestion of doubt, and immediately added: "However, I do not think so. One of his books once fell into my hands; I opened it, and hit upon the following: 'The Russian peasant cuts down a whole oak in order that he may make himself a cart-shaft or an axle from a bough.' Then I shut the book and said to myself: 'I've had enough of Melnikoff.'"

One may not agree with some of Lyeff Nikolaevitch's assertions about books and people. But I have never chanced to observe that he exhibited a sarcastic, malicious feeling toward any one, or that the opinions expressed by him were tinged with the color of his relations toward the people. Thus, while he always bore himself with particular warmth toward Lyeskoff and N. Strakhoff, as men, both during their lifetime and after their death, he invariably said that there was a good-sized spoonful of tar in their cask of honey.[1] This independence in his judgments, and the sincere straightforwardness with which L. N. Tolstoy bears himself toward everything, always impart to his words a peculiar value.

[1] A Russian proverb, "A spoonful of tar in a cask of honey," indicating that a very little of a bad thing will spoil a great deal of a good thing. — Tr.

CHAPTER XVI

Lyeff Nikolaevitch's constant aspiration toward veracity and lucidity in his writings demands much time, not only in the writing itself, but also in the preparatory work. He tries to find in life the confirmation of the situations which he has invented, and immediately rejects everything imaginary when life furnishes a ready-made episode. This was the case with *Anna Karenina*, whom L. N. Tolstoy did not, at first, intend to kill. But an analogous romantic episode happened near Yasnaya Polyana, where the unhappy heroine, Anna, threw herself under the railway train. This impelled L. N. Tolstoy to a fresh treatment of the question, and considerably modified his original plan.

Anna Karenina was begun under the following circumstances. One evening, in 1873, Lyeff Nikolaevitch entered the drawing-room as his eldest son, Sergyeĭ, was reading aloud to his wife *Byelkin's Story*, by Pushkin. The reading ceased when Lyeff Nikolaevitch made his appearance. He asked what they were reading and opened the book, and when he read, "The guests assembled at the country-house," he went into ecstasies.

"That is the way one ought always to begin to write!" said he. "That immediately arouses the reader's interest."

A relative of the Tolstoys declared that it would be a very good thing if L. N. T. would write a novel of high life. That evening Lyeff Nikolaevitch wrote, "Everything was in a tumult at the house of the Oblonskys."

And then, when he began to write the romance, he placed at the beginning: "All happy families resemble each other; every unhappy family is unhappy after its own fashion."

The Death of Ivan Ilitch was written by Lyeff Nikolaevitch under the influence of a narration by one of the members of the Moscow Court, concerning the death of his comrade, Ivan Ilitch M.

The Kreutzer Sonata had its origin in the following circumstances. The artist I. Ryépin, and the actor Andreeff-Burlak, who made Lyeff Nikolaevitch laugh until he ached with his amusing stories, were visiting at Yasnaya Polyana, and one evening, Mme. G., who had just arrived from abroad, played the *Kreutzer Sonata* with such brilliant expressiveness, that she produced upon every one, and, in particular, upon Lyeff Nikolaevitch, a very profound impression, under the influence of which he said to I. Ryépin: —

"Let us write *The Kreutzer Sonata.* You with the brush, I with the pen, and Vasily Nikolaevitch (Andreeff-Burlak) shall read it on the stage, where your picture shall stand."

This proposal called forth general approbation.

After a time, Lyeff Nikolaevitch, with his characteristic perseverance, set to work at what, probably, had long been seething in his brain.

The Power of Darkness was taken, in its entirety, from a case in court which occurred in Tula.

The Fruits of Civilization was written for amateur theatricals at Yasnaya Polyana. At first the play consisted of two acts, and was called *She was crafty.* But as the rehearsals, in which Lyeff Nikolaevitch took an active part, proceeded, he improved and amplified the piece, in conformity with the number of the acting personages. During the performance of the play, several of the actors gave him so much pleasure by their acting that some of the scenes were forever graven on his memory. He was especially enthusiastic over his examining magistrate, L., who took the part of one of the peasants.

"He came to Yasnaya Polyana," Lyeff Nikolaevitch relates, "and all day long he hardly spoke to any one, but kept walking about with drooping head. But on the stage he surpassed them all, and out of his small part he made something so fine that I had not even foreseen it when I wrote that part."

And, growing animated, according to his custom when true genius is under discussion, Lyeff Nikolaevitch began to recall the playing of the old Moscow actors: Shstchepkin, Martynoff, and others. He expressed himself with particular warmth about Martynoff: —

"He was a great artist," said he, "uniting in himself three precious qualities: talent, wit, and the capacity for persistent labor. In A. Potyekhin's play, *Stolen Goods bring no Luck*, Martynoff was so incomparable, that I, although I was only then beginning my literary career, started the applause, and we organized an ovation for him."

And when Lyeff Nikolaevitch said this, his face lost its stern character, and kindled with the youthful, captivating flame of enthusiasm.

I chanced to behold L. N. Tolstoy a second time in that state during April of last year, when the talented sculptor, Prince P. Trubetskoy, was in Moscow, having come thither from Italy, where he always lives. Prince Trubetskoy expressed a desire to make a bust of Lyeff Nikolaevitch. When I came to Tolstoy, the bust had been begun, and was standing in the dining-room, downstairs, covered with damp cloths.

"You have not heard of the sculptor, Trubetskoy?" asked Lyeff Nikolaevitch, as he bade me welcome.

"No."

"Then come with me and I will show you something. What wonderful talent!" said L. N., becoming animated. And with swift, lively steps, he led me to the lower dining-room, striding down several steps of the staircase at a time. In the dining-room Lyeff Nikolaevitch went up to the veiled bust, and, without ceasing to talk animatedly about Prince P. Trubetskoy's exceptional talent, he began, with irresolute mien, to free the bust from the damp cloths. And, in fact, even from the work which Prince Trubetskoy had done in a few hours, it was possible to judge of this sculptor's remarkable talent. Before me were two Lyeff Tolstoys:

one living, speaking, impressionable; the other speechless, motionless, but as familiar to me as the first.

With profound feeling I divided my attention between the superb work of man and the master-creation of nature, that had sent forth so splendid and artistic a temperament, which, at the age of seventy, can flame so infectiously with the fire of pure ecstasy.

CHAPTER XVII

The hot and passionate temperament wherewith nature endowed L. N. Tolstoy has not been destroyed by outward influences to the present time. One day, not long ago, a horse grew restive under him. He is a good horseman, and loves horses after the manner of a coachman — carefully and tenderly, and understands capitally how to manage them. He knows their nature, their habits, and their tricks, and sometimes it even seems as though he understood their language. But, in this case, nothing was of any avail. The horse reared and backed. All at once, Lyeff Nikolaevitch straightened up, his eyes flashed, and the whip descended, hissing through the air, upon the horse. The horse sprang forward, and a minute later no one would have believed that this plainly garbed, modest old man, with a white beard, could be so menacing. But one thing may be asserted with truth, that this affair did not pass off without leaving its traces upon Lyeff Nikolaevitch, for, with his hot temperament, and pugnacious, self-willed character, he at the same time possesses a remarkably sensitive conscience, which suffers tortures at every act of violence.

In this chain of seething, imperious instincts linked with delicate spiritual organization lies the profound tragicness of Tolstoy's personality. Born with strong passions, and with a character in the highest degree elastic, mettlesome, and self-willed, presenting in his person in every respect man raised, as it were, to the cube, or that "over-man" (*übermensch*) of whom Nietszche dreamed, L. N. Tolstoy at the same time possesses an all-embracing soul, which thirsts for self-perfection. On the one hand, an insatiable thirst for power over people, and on the other, an unconquerable ardor for inward purity and the sweetness of meekness.

Prometheus, in the aspect of a stooping river-boatman with his hauling-noose around his neck, or some Caius Marcius Coriolanus, in the position of a servant, would present a less tragical situation. What a theme for a psychological drama! Yet this tragic state is a characteristic peculiarity of the Tolstoy personality, and gleams forth in nearly all his writings.

The elements of this tragedy lie in his religious zeal, which can never reconcile the man with himself, and keeps his soul constantly in a state of powerful tension, — "like fish on dry land," to use the characteristic expression of the Danish thinker, Kierkegaard.

This aspiration to become from finite infinite, from ashes the Phœnix, from "the bag of meat" God, this aspiration which lies, in potential form, in every writer, is developed in L. N. Tolstoy to the highest degree, and constitutes, as it were, his second nature. Turgeneff, as far back as the '50's, wrote to Druzhinin concerning L. Tolstoy: "When this young wine shall have got through fermenting, there will come forth from it a beverage worthy of the gods." But what Turgeneff did not divine, because he was lacking in religious experience, was that the man who believes can never "get through fermenting," and drop the curtain upon his inner world. Life every day creates some fresh complication, and imposes fresh burdens upon him. L. N. Tolstoy will never free himself from burdens of this sort. He finds it especially painful in Moscow, where his life is not always arranged according to his plans, and he is often compelled to dwell in a sphere that is alien to him.

One day he met one of his visitors on the street, and got into conversation with him. It appeared that this man lived in bachelor quarters, dined where he pleased, and could, at any time, isolate himself in Moscow as in an uninhabited island.

Lyeff Nikolaevitch told about this meeting, and added with a smile: —

"And I envied him to a degree which I am ashamed

to express. Just think of it: a man can live *as he likes* without causing suffering to any one. Really, that is — bliss!"

The conversation turned upon the imperative necessity for solitude in the case of certain people, and the burdensomeness of isolation for others, who would undergo any sort of suffering rather than solitude. Some one cited the instance of a doctor who went mad after two months of solitary confinement.

"Yes, yes, that may be," said Lyeff Nikolaevitch. "But, on the other hand, solitude may be genuine bliss for people who are able to draw resources from within themselves."

"Voluntary, yes; but involuntary, no," said some one.

"Why? everything depends on the man's relation to certain phenomena," returned Lyeff Nikolaevitch. "They tell a story about a certain gentleman who, for some reason, was kept for a long time in solitary confinement, and spent his time there in a very remarkable manner. He managed it as follows: he evoked in his memory the recollections which were dear to him, visited, in thought, all his friends, and held with them prolonged conversations on the most varied topics. Thus his time passed; he enjoyed an excellent state of mind, and good sleep. But is there nothing except imaginary conversations of which a man can think, when he is left alone? Especially in later years, when the animal life has considerably calmed down, and problems of the spirit have come to the front. Then it often happens that it is a hardship to be with people who are strangers to him. Solitude at that time of life is not a hardship, but a delight, a happiness of which one can only dream. Some people wonder at Socrates who died and did not care to flee from prison. But is it not better to die consciously in fulfilment of one's duty, than unexpectedly from some stupid bacteria? And I have always been surprised that so clever a man as Turgeneff should bear himself as he did toward death. He was awfully afraid of death. Is it even incomprehensible that he was not *afraid to be afraid of death?* And that darkness of reason was really astonishing in him! He and Prince L'D. D. Urusoff used to discuss religion, and Turgeneff used to dispute and dispute, and all of a sudden he would no longer be able to control himself, and would cover up his ears, and, pretending that he had forgotten Urusoff's name, would shout, 'I won't listen any longer to that Prince Trubetzkoy.'"

And L. N. Tolstoy mimicked Turgeneff's voice until one would have thought the man was there [illegible]. When he is in good humor, and finds himself [illegible] circle of [illegible] friends, he [illegible]

HOUSE OF COUNT TOLSTOY AT YASNAYA POLYANA

[illegible] a man [illegible] as he likes [illegible] Really, that is

[illegible] upon the [illegible] the [illegible] certain [illegible] the [illegible] of [illegible] who would un[illegible] any sort of suffering [illegible] Some [illegible] cited the instance [illegible] went mad after two months of solitary [illegible]

"Yes, yes, [illegible] Lyeff Nikolaevitch. "But, on the other [illegible] may be genuine bliss for people who are able to draw resources from within themselves."

"Voluntary, yes; but involuntary, no," said some one.

"Why? everything depends on the man's relation to certain phenomena," returned Lyeff Nikolaevitch. "They tell a story about a certain gentleman who, for some reason, was kept for a long time in solitary confinement, and spent his time there in a very remarkable manner. He managed it as follows: he evoked in his memory the recollections which were dear to him, visited in thought all his friends and held with them pro[illegible] Thus [illegible] mind, [illegible] ordinary [illegible] left [illegible] animal life [illegible] the [illegible] happens that it is a hardship to be with people who are strangers to him. Solitude at that time of life is not a hardship, but a delight, a happiness of which one can only dream. Some people wonder at Socrates who died and did not care to flee from prison. But is it not better to die consciously in fulfilment of one's duty, than unexpectedly from some stupid bacteria? And I have always been surprised that so clever a man as Turgeneff should bear himself as he did toward death. He was awfully afraid of death. Is it even incomprehensible that he was not *afraid to be afraid of death?* And that darkness of reason was really astonishing in him! He and Prince D. D. Urusoff used to discuss religion, and Turgeneff used to dispute and dispute, and all of a sudden he would no longer be able to control himself, and would cover up his ears, and, pretending that he had forgotten Urusoff's name, would shout, 'I won't listen any longer to that Prince Trubetzkoy.'"

And L. N. Tolstoy mimicked Turgeneff's voice until one would have thought the man was there in person. When he is in good humor, and finds himself in the circle of his intimate friends, he sometimes communicates his impressions of persons, and accurately discriminates the characteristic peculiarities of each individual.

CHAPTER XVIII

WITH the spring flitting of the Tolstoys from Moscow to Yasnaya Polyana, Lyeff Nikolaevitch's life is fitted into a more convenient frame. In the first place, the country, with its conditions of life, and the absence of constant tragic contrasts, has a favorable action upon Lyeff Nikolaevitch; in the second place, at Yasnaya Polyana he has more time at his disposal, although the "spectators" do not let him alone even there.

Yasnaya Polyana descended to L. N. Tolstoy from his mother, by birth a Princess Volkhonsky, whom he has immortalized in *War and Peace*, under the name of Princess Marya Bolkonsky. It is proper to mention that the name *Lyeff* was given to him in honor of her former betrothed, Prince Lyeff Golitzin, who had died.

L. N. Tolstoy was born at Yasnaya Polyana, August 28 (September 9, N.S.), 1828. But the house in which our great writer first saw the light now belongs to other owners and stands in another village.

When he was in the Caucasus, at the beginning of the '50's, Lyeff Nikolaevitch found himself in difficult financial circumstances, in consequence of a heavy loss at cards, so he commissioned one of his relatives to sell the house for removal. And the vast manor-house, with its pillars and verandas, was sold for about five thousand rubles. At the present time, no one lives in the house, and it stands in the village of Dolgoe, neglected, and with the windows boarded up.

I visited the house in February of the present year, with an amateur photographer, P. V. Preobrazhensky. A feeling of oppression seized upon us, when, balancing ourselves on the cross-beams, we entered the half-ruined house, with its projecting balconies, crumbling walls, and heaps of rubbish, where young life had for-

merly beamed and throbbed abundantly. A piercing wind rushed through the boarded-up windows, and raised clouds of dust. In the corner room, where was born the "great writer of the Russian land," lay a disordered mass of broken fragments, and a pile of various odds and ends.

Of the former decoration, all that remained was bits of the ornaments here and there. But the lower story, where the school-room had been, and where the famous Karl Ivanitch had been used to tickle his pupil's heels, is still sound and fit for habitation.

The first time I was at Yasnaya Polyana was in the autumn of 1895.

It was a clear, cool morning when the train of the Moscow-Kursk railway halted at the station of "Kozloffzasyeka," which is three versts from Yasnaya Polyana. The road from the station here runs through a broad cutting in the oak forest, which was already touched with autumnal hues, and stood out picturesquely against the pale turquoise sky.

I was driven in a cabriolet by a broad-shouldered coachman, with a black beard, shaven on the cheeks. He talked in a dignified way, and expressed his approbation of his employers. Lyeff Nikolaevitch particularly pleased him.

"There can be no such other gentleman in the world as Lyeff Nikolaevitch," said he. "He seems to be not more important, but less important, than every one else. And whoever is there, be it a general or a common man, he makes no distinction whatever. He is the same with every one — courteous, sociable. The Countess is a good lady, also, but of another sort; she 's terribly fond of order."

We crossed the macadam highway, straight as an arrow, and perceived, on the slope of an elevation, a large park, which concealed from us Yasnaya Polyana. The park, laid out at Yasnaya Polyana during Lyeff Nikolaevitch's period of enthusiasm for rural affairs, is very large. It occupies about thirty desyatins,[1] and

[1] Eighty-one acres.

during the harvest season there is an immense amount of apples.

At the entrance to the Yasnaya Polyana park stand two towers, in medieval style, placed there by L. N. Tolstoy's grandfather on his mother's side, N. S. Volkhonsky. From these towers the road runs through the park, rising a little as it approaches the house, and forms a level corridor through the aged birches. Through the dense leaves gleamed a pond, and glimpses were visible of a square, smoothly rolled space, with a net for lawn-tennis, and at last shone out in its whiteness the long, two-story house where the greater part of Lyeff Tolstoy's life has been passed. This house was not built all at once, but, as it were, spread out in proportion as the family increased.

The cabriolet drove round the side of the house, which is devoid of windows, and halted before a low porch, toward which an ancient elm tree, called here the *poor people's tree*, stretched forth its many-branched trunk. Beside the elm stands the bench on which the poor people and the peasants await Lyeff Nikolaevitch. In a small vestibule, with an unpainted floor, stood a broad bookcase, filled with books, chiefly by foreign authors. By the side of the mirror, with its letter-box, shone two bicycles, and a long box with the implements for croquet was to be seen. On the pier-glass lay two bundles of English journals, with a multitude of stamps, and a Japanese journal, with vertical lines. A broad wooden staircase ascended from the vestibule. Here, as in Moscow, everything had an air of simplicity, long use, and the solidity of the ancient gentry.

The lackey who came out to meet me from behind a partition-wall, with his little daughter, welcomed me cordially, and said that Lyeff Nikolaevitch was up-stairs with guests.

This was contrary to rules. Generally he sets great value on the morning. I entered a very large hall, with windows on both sides, and hung with time-blackened family portraits. In the center of the room, at a long table, sat Lyeff Nikolaevitch and several guests. It was about nine o'clock in the morning. On the table stood a boiling samovar, with coffee-cups, cream, bread, and butter.

Lyeff Nikolaevitch had grown somewhat older during the time since I had last seen him. His gray hair had grown thinner, his beard had become longer and whiter. He was chatting with a student, chewing bread, and moving his chin back and forth.

After introducing me to his visitors, and talking for a few minutes, Lyeff Nikolaevitch rose, poured himself out a cup of barley coffee, and, excusing himself, went to his own room to work. But he halted near the door, and said to the student: —

"And, later on, you will be surprised that the philosophical course can give you nothing. Well, you will learn what a certain Terence wrote, when he was of the same age. But, really now, what do you want of it?"

The student said quietly, and as though ashamed of his frivolity, that he had been drawn into the philosophical course by a liking for that science.

Lyeff Nikolaevitch hastily acknowledged the legitimate character of this inclination, and, with a friendly nod, went off down-stairs, shuffling his feet. But it sometimes happens that he stands near that door for hours together, with a cup or glass in his hand. So that place is called the *Enchanted Spot*, because Lyeff Nikolaevitch often enters into conversation with some one on his path, imperceptibly is carried away with the subject of conversation, and stands by the hour near the door.

CHAPTER XIX

THE Countess, her daughters, relatives who had arrived from Kieff, an Englishwoman, a Frenchwoman, a student-tutor, the boys and their comrades, began to assemble in the dining-room. All entered separately, drank their coffee or their tea, and went off about their own affairs. Others appeared to take their place, made a litter of bread crumbs, left the tea-pot half filled, and the coffee-pot cold, and departed.

With the appearance of Countess Sophia Andreevna, order was perceptibly restored. The extinguished samovar began to sing, the cold coffce was heated, the overbrewed tea was replaced with fresh tea. Sophia Andreevna is a capital housewife, attentive, hospitable. One eats and drinks at Yasnaya Polyana as at home.

All the complicated and troublesome management of the housekeeping and the direction of business is under the charge of Sophia Andreevna. She is indefatigable, and brings her brisk energy, thriftiness, and activity to bear on everything. Not without cause did the coachman say that the Countess "was terribly fond of order." She has only to go away for a day or two on business from Yasnaya Polyana, and the complicated machine called "the household" begins to creak and jolt.

The Countess has no helpers. Her three eldest sons live apart, and each is busy with his own affairs. Her daughters have their own interests and duties, which occupy every moment of their time. L. N. Tolstoy's eldest daughter, Tatyana Lvovna, in particular, a girl of exceptional talent, has been working very hard of late. In addition to the hurried copying of her father's articles, she conducts his vast correspondence.

Lyeff Nikolaevitch Tolstoy could not answer with his own hand all the letters he receives, even if he had four hands. A mass of letters is received from all quarters of the globe, and in all sorts of languages.

Who all does not address himself to him with greetings, with sympathy, with poignant problems, and accusations? Young Russians and Frenchmen, Americans, Dutchmen, Poles, Englishmen, Baroness Bertha Suttner, and a devout Brahmin from India, the dying Turgeneff, and the highwayman Tchurkin, writing like a wounded wild beast.

The vastness of Lyeff Nikolaevitch's correspondence may be judged from the fact that letters concerning the Famine Year alone occupy a whole cupboard. Letters are kept at the Tolstoys' in foreign fashion with the envelopes in which they are received, and rarely does a letter remain unanswered.

After coffee, all hastily departed about their own affairs, and the hall was deserted. I went down-stairs to the library, which, with the adjoining room, is assigned to guests.

This room is furnished plainly but tastefully; one feels very comfortable in it, and very much at home. On the wall hang family portraits, also portraits of Dickens, Schopenhauer, Turgeneff, E. Kovalevsky, and others. In the center of the wall, in a niche, stands a small marble bust of Lyeff Nikolaevitch's favorite brother, Count Nikolaï Tolstoy, whom I have already mentioned. The lower drawing-room is separated from the library by a yellow wooden partition, with a crossbeam which once suggested to L. N. Tolstoy thoughts of suicide, during the period of his spiritual wanderings.

One wall in the library is chiefly occupied by gifts from authors. And what dedications are there! In prose, and in verse, in Italian, and in Servian, turgid, and modest, and of every sort.

One room beyond the library is Lyeff Nikolaevitch's study, a small room, with an unpainted floor, a vaulted ceiling, and thick stone walls. Formerly it was a storeroom, and on the ceiling, to this day, are heavy, black iron rings, on which, in their day, hams used to hang, and which were afterward employed by Lyeff Nikolaevitch for gymnastic exercise.

It is as cool and quiet in the study as in a cellar. The furnishing of the Yasnaya Polyana study differs from that in Moscow in this — that here are various implements of labor: a scythe, a saw, pincers, files, and others. At first all this appears to be "affectation," but when one lives in the country, one becomes convinced that all this is absolutely indispensable; and one must, imperatively, know how to do everything himself, in order not to fall constantly into a dependent and helpless position.

CHAPTER XX

At three o'clock, Lyeff Nikolaevitch looked into the library, and proposed to me to take a walk before dinner. His face was weary, with sunken cheeks, but animated. His eyes still shone with the waning fire of excited thought. Because of the cool weather, he wore a threadbare cloth pelerine, and a woolen cap of domestic manufacture. But these garments did not become him at all, and one could feel reconciled to them only because of their usefulness. However, after the lapse of a few minutes, it seemed as though he ought to be in precisely that attire.

Lyeff Nikolaevitch had hardly made his appearance, when several persons quitted the *poor people's tree* and approached the porch.

"Good day. What's the matter?" inquired Lyeff Nikolaevitch, quietly, but with a curt, businesslike tone, thrusting his staff under his arm, and unfolding a document which a peasant had handed to him.

The man began incoherently to explain some law case. Lyeff Nikolaevitch listened to him for a while, with concentrated attention, and kept repeating:—

"Just so, just so."

Then, evidently having formed a clear idea of what the peasant wanted, he thrust the document into his pocket, and promised to do all that was necessary, that is, to write a complaint to the Court of Appeal.

Another peasant, of small stature, ill-favored, with shifty eyes, held by the hand a pale, scrofulous little boy, and stared intently at him. Evidently, according to the program already prepared, the boy was expected to move Lyeff Nikolaevitch to compassion in some way. But the boy had become confused, and hung back. Lyeff Nikolaevitch asked the peasant what he wanted. The man began to talk quickly, in general terms, about his hard life, and then brought the conversation round to the extreme need of wood. Lyeff Nikolaevitch promised to make inquiries about the wood, and to aid his petitioner in this matter. Two young men approached, clad in full trousers, sunburnt of countenance and with a southern accent. They were excavators, and were working several versts distant from Yasnaya Polyana. They had heard of "the good gentleman," and had come for some little books.

"For what little books?" asked Lyeff Nikolaevitch.

One of the young fellows, with an embroidered shirt, said, with an easy manner, that they wanted good little books to read, and they especially wished to read *God's World.*

Lyeff Nikolaevitch replied that he had no such book. But the young fellow insisted that he must have it, because one of the excavators had spoken of it. Lyeff Nikolaevitch went to his study, and found a collection of all sorts of scientific information, under the general title of *The Secrets and Marvels of God's World.* He gave them the book, and requested them to bring it back in good condition. The young man turned over the leaves with curiosity, and assured Lyeff Nikolaevitch that he might rest easy. We were about to set out, when from behind the house appeared a masculine figure, in a cap with a red band, and in a threadbare overcoat. The aspect of the stranger did not inspire confidence. He made a theatrical salute from afar, and with a theatrical gesture pulled from his pocket a document.

"A certificate of my personal character."

"It is not necessary — not necessary," said Lyeff Nikolaevitch, hastily, casting a quick glance at the stranger, and beat a retreat into the porch.

A minute later he returned, and, endeavoring not to look at the stranger, thrust something into his hand. The man returned thanks, but, evidently, was not satisfied with what he had received. Then he drew still another paper from his pocket. "Here is a certificate, your Illustrious Highness —"

"I have given you what I could, I am not able to do

more," said Lyeff Nikolaevitch, with an expression of martyrdom.

And we set off through the park. But the ugly little peasant and his scrofulous boy intercepted our path. Lyeff Nikolaevitch halted.

"What do you want?"

The peasant thrust forward the boy. The boy hesitated, became agitated, and, drawling out his words, appealed to Lyeff Nikolaevitch: —

"Gi-i-i-ve the co-o-o-olt —"

I felt uncomfortable, and knew not in which direction to look.

Lyeff Nikolaevitch shrugged his shoulders.

"What colt? What nonsense? I have no colt."

"Yes, you have," declared the ill-favored little peasant, moving briskly forward.

"Well, I know nothing about it. Go, and God be with you!" said Lyeff Nikolaevitch, and, taking several strides, he leaped over a ditch.

We walked at a brisk gait in the fields, first through the rye, and then along the water-meadows, which gleamed cheerfully in the sunshine with their succulent verdure.

Lyeff Nikolaevitch began to question me about my life in the country. The conversation turned on the rearing of children. L. N. Tolstoy is opposed to the existing educational institutions, and thinks that they take away from the children much more than they give them. He quoted, jestingly, the remark of one of his friends, who is educating his son at home, and always says that, if his son does turn out a fool, at all events, he will not be a choke-full fool such as comes out of the Gymnasium.

But Lyeff Nikolaevitch himself and his life interested me more than anything else. At what was he working? How does he live? What are his relations to the people, and, especially, to those Makaroffs and Morozoffs who once constituted the famous literary firm, — "Makaroff, Morozoff, Tolstoy?" And I led the conversation to that subject.

Lyeff Nikolaevitch, gliding swiftly over the ground,

soft as a carpet, said that he felt very well, except that lately he had fallen ill with his usual complaint — in the liver. He was occupied at the time with a very complicated piece of work, which entirely engrossed him. He was interested in those three steps through which the spirit of man must infallibly move onward to perfection. And Lyeff Nikolaevitch began with animation to set forth the fundamental theses of his work: —

The first step is warfare with a false view of the world. This must be the beginning.

The second step is warfare with delusion, that is to say, with phenomena which conduce to abnormal life; and in conclusion,

The third step is warfare against sin.

From warfare with abnormal phenomena, the conversation passed naturally to the melancholy side of the common people's life, and I questioned Lyeff Nikolaevitch about the Yasnaya Polyana peasants, as to what sort of people they were.

"They are peasants like any other peasants," said he, "not much better, not much worse, than the rest. With some of them I long ago established kindly, affectionate relations, and they are maintained to this day, others — and they are in the majority — look upon me as a sort of horn of plenty, and that is all. And can one expect from them any other relations? Their life and views have been formed through a course of ages under the influence of a multitude of irresistible conditions. And can one change all that?"

We came out upon the road, and met an old woman who was on her way to Yasnaya Polyana. On catching sight of Lyeff Nikolaevitch she came to a standstill. He entered into conversation with her about her mode of life, gave her alms, and we again turned out of the road into the fields. Lyeff Nikolaevitch interrupted the conversation only for a moment, and, glancing round, he admired the golden attire of the autumn.

Suddenly, through the transparent air, from the direction of the house, resounded the prolonged and persistent sound of a bell.

"They are summoning us to dinner," said Lyeff Nikolaevitch, and quickened his pace, without, however, breaking off the conversation.

We went straight ahead, leaping across gullies and puddles, which had formed after the rain. It was the first time I had made such a forced march with Lyeff Nikolaevitch, and I felt involuntary surprise at the elastic lightness with which he surmounted all obstacles. He seemed not to walk, but to glide over the ground, evidently without making any particular effort. I mentally compared him with writers of my acquaintance, who were much younger than he, and they appeared to me like ruins in comparison with him, so far as their physical and mental endurance were concerned: how much fire and force there is in him yet!

And it is not astonishing, for after C. Lombroso had been at Yasnaya Polyana, he said that L. Tolstoy was fit to be his son, in the matter of freshness, and then L. N. Tolstoy called Lombroso, in jest, "an amiable old man," although the latter is much younger than Lyeff Nikolaevitch. One episode of C. Lombroso's sojourn at Yasnaya Polyana is not devoid of interest. They went to take a bath. Lyeff Nikolaevitch asked C. Lombroso whether he knew how to swim. The latter declared that he did, watched Lyeff Nikolaevitch, and faithfully imitated everything that the latter did. L. N. Tolstoy crawled out on the outer board, sprang into the water, and swam off. C. Lombroso followed him.

"But I turned round," says Lyeff Nikolaevitch, "and saw that my old man was floundering about in the water, but, somehow, was making no progress."

L. N. helped him to get out. Lombroso was panting, but in ecstasies over his bath. In order to warm himself up after his bath, Lyeff Nikolaevitch raised himself several times by his muscles. Lombroso, also, clung to the cross-beam, but could not raise himself. His visit gave L. N. Tolstoy great pleasure.

"I had imagined him to be different — a scientific fanatic," said L. N. afterward. "He is nothing of the sort."

CHAPTER XXI

WHEN we reached the house, the large bell, suspended from a dead limb of the *poor people's tree*, had rung insistently for the second time. It was three o'clock.[1] We arrived exactly in time. Immediately after us appeared the servant with the soup-tureen in his hands.

The long table quickly filled up with Lyeff Nikolaevitch's numerous family, and Countess Sophia Andreevna greeted our prompt arrival with a glance of approbation,

She occupied the so-called housewife's place; that is, at the end of the table, so that she could see everything and everybody. Next her, on her right, sat Lyeff Nikolaevitch, and beside him his eldest daughter, Tatyana Lvovna. This order is preserved at dinner always and everywhere.

Lyeff Nikolaevitch and his two oldest daughters eat no meat, and separate dishes are served for them. Lyeff Nikolaevitch often plays the part of host in the little vegetarian nook. He ladles out the thin oatmeal gruel into plates, and cordially helps vegetarian guests during the dinner, now to one dish, now to another.

He is a vegetarian from conviction, and for many years has eaten neither meat nor fish, but attributes great importance to vegetable diet, both from a physiological and from an esthetic point of view. And, of course, he might serve as an eloquent example of the superiority of vegetable diet, if it were only possible to prove that the fine strength which he enjoys depends principally on his vegetable diet. In any case this is a serious question. And a man who lives exclusively on a vegetable diet, and, at the same time, is able, at the age of seventy, to fulfil, in thorough fashion, the field labor of the peas-

[1] An error somewhere, evidently, about the hour of the walk and of dinner. The dinner hour at Yasnaya Polyana is nearer five o'clock. — TR.

ants, to ride scores of versts on his bicycle, to play for hours at lawn-tennis, or to run races with the little boys, — such a man has a good deal of right to talk about the superiority of a vegetable diet.

Countess Sophia Andreevna, on the contrary, opposes a vegetable diet, and only tolerates it in the house as, in a way, her cross. But justice must be accorded to her impartiality: the meat viands and the vegetarian viands at Yasnaya Polyana are very savory, nutritious, and varied.

Lyeff Nikolaevitch, in many respects, reminds one of a Russian peasant, but he does not eat like a Russian peasant, — with their deliberation and pauses, — but quickly and hastily, as though in a hurry to get rid, as soon as possible, of a disagreeable duty.

After the first course, with which he had dulled the edge of his hunger, Lyeff Nikolaevitch began to address remarks first to one, then to another, of those present, imparting to the most trivial conversation that peculiar, rich interest which he understands how to infuse into everything. His humorous comments often evoked peals of laughter, which were especially loud at the other end of the table, where the youngest of the young people are always grouped.

Occasionally, when relating something, Lyeff Nikolaevitch, on hearing laughter among the young people, interrupted his narration, and turned his attention in that direction. But, without fail, in the course of the dinner, he scrutinized all with his keen glance, and exchanged at least a few words with every individual.

At the Tolstoys' table we drank home-brewed grain, *kvas*, cold milk, and soda-water.

But immediately after dinner Lyeff Nikolaevitch suggested a stroll in the forest, and began to urge the ladies to haste. He is impatient in such circumstances, and does not like long preparations. But some one proposed a game of lawn-tennis while all were assembling. Lyeff Nikolaevitch willingly assented.

And, a moment later, male and female figures were flitting about over the hard-rolled square space in front of the house, flourishing rackets, and shouting, with a tinge of anger, "Play!" "Out!" and so forth.

Lawn-tennis is, as we all know, one of the most fascinating of games, requiring keenness of sight, skill, and the exercise of every muscle. And it is easily comprehensible that Lyeff Nikolaevitch is passionately fond of this game; it affords considerable work for his muscles. He plays ardently and with fire, but without losing his temper. This constant work upon himself is to be felt even in a game of lawn-tennis.

Once he even yielded his racket to another player, at the most interesting moment of the game. However, this was an exceptional case.

CHAPTER XXII

As he was raising himself by his muscles one day, during the morning bath, he broke down, somehow, and fell between the boards of the bath-house, causing himself considerable injuries to the breast and back. It all took place so quickly that neither the doctor, who was present, nor I succeeded in recovering from our fright and going to the assistance of Lyeff Nikolaevitch. He crawled out, unaided, from the crevice, and looked around in amazement, unable to understand how it had all happened. The right side of his breast and back were covered with dark red blotches. The doctor, shaking his head reproachfully, began to massage the injured parts, and to inquire concerning the degree of pain.

L. N. Tolstoy stood patiently, his body shivering with the cold water, and kept repeating, with a smile:—

"It is nothing, really — it hurts only a little."

"And here?"

"Well, here it does seem to be painful. And how could it have happened?" he asked in surprise, and as though excusing himself to the doctor and to me for the unpleasant scene.

But, in the opinion of the doctor, Lyeff Nikolaevitch ought to have experienced burning pains. He felt chilled in the air, and began to dress himself, advising us to go on ahead, because he intended to walk fast in order to get warm. Of course, we did not follow his advice.

When he had dressed himself, and thrown his towel round his neck, he really did set off at rapid pace up the hill, without heeding the doctor's warning that at such a time all quick movements should be avoided. We could hardly keep up with him. It was particularly difficult for the doctor, who was rather fat and suffered from asthma. On observing this, Lyeff Nikolaevitch slackened his pace, and began to talk about a letter which he had received, the day before, from a Polish Count, who was trying to entice him with Polish patriotism. After quoting the contents of the letter, Lyeff Nikolaevitch said:—

"How often the checkers get mixed up in political matters! Great caution is required, or one will find himself in a false position. It often happens that people who have no inward bond between them march hand in hand under one flag — under the flag of a common hatred. What a sorry bond is that! And what lack of understanding that love alone can cement men, and give them true strength."

And Lyeff Nikolaevitch went on talking about love, as the indispensable element in every alliance. When we entered the dining-room he quickly ate his morning oatmeal, hastily looked over the English newspaper — the *Daily Chronicle* — poured himself out half a cup of coffee with almond milk, on his way, and excusing himself, hastily went off to his own rooms.

"He certainly must be suffering torments now," said the doctor, nodding approvingly in the direction of Lyeff Nikolaevitch.

That day, Lyeff Nikolaevitch emerged only to dinner, and all the time he was so animated and merry that no one would have said that his back and a part of his breast were one mass of bruises. After dinner, the doctor began to insist that he should again be allowed to massage the injured places.

"Well, if you like!" said Lyeff Nikolaevitch, evidently not wishing to pain the doctor by a refusal, and he led him off to his study.

When the doctor laid bare the bruised parts, he shook his head. A part of the breast and back had assumed a purplish brown hue, with an iridescent play of colors. The doctor greased his hand with vaseline, and began to pass it delicately over the body, as though pressing out the pain from the wounded portions of the skin.

Lyeff Nikolaevitch lay motionless, never ceasing to talk, and highly approving the doctor's work.

"How well you do that!"

But the doctor wore a stern aspect, and kept repeating, persistently, in rhythm with the movement of his hand: —

"The principal thing now is to avoid violent mo-o-ovement; the principal thing is to give the irritated ti-i-issues rest."

Lyeff Nikolaevitch made no reply.

But when, half an hour later, the doctor arrived at the lawn-tennis ground, he saw, among the players, Lyeff Nikolaevitch, who was flourishing his racket with animation. The doctor sat down heavily on a bench, and waved his hand in despair. Lyeff Nikolaevitch caught his glance of displeasure, and hastily handed over his racket.

"I won't do it; I won't do it any more," he said, in a guilty tone, and went up to the doctor.

CHAPTER XXIII

Countess Sophia Andreevna had finished all her domestic arrangements, and made her appearance, with the other ladies, near the lawn-tennis ground.

Lyeff Nikolaevitch began to urge the players to haste, and, a few minutes later, a company of twelve persons set out straight across the park. Lyeff Nikolaevitch conducted the expedition. We went up hill and down, made our way through the thicket, crossed the water on a transverse plank. Lyeff Nikolaevitch was merry, and animated, and talkative; he helped the ladies at difficult points, and even invented for one lady something in the nature of an elevator: he pressed the head of his staff against the back of her belt, and thereby considerably lightened the ascent for her.

When, at last, we emerged into an open spot, before us lay outspread a rather picturesque view, with yellowing groups of trees, effectively lighted up by the rays of the setting sun. Here and there, stately, dark green fir trees stood out, sharply outlined against the golden background of the autumn foliage. We turned aside to the nursery of forest trees, inspected them, and took a path for the macadamized highway. Lyeff Nikolaevitch took an interest in everything, entered into conversation with every one, and exchanged friendly greetings with every one whom we met, without waiting for them to bow to him. In all, we traversed about seven versts. Toward the end of the walk, all felt somewhat weary and thirsty.

The samovar was already boiling in the dining-room, and the cups gleamed cheerfully. Lyeff Nikolaevitch took a new number of the *Revue de Paris*, which had just arrived, and went to his study. It is a genuine

COUNT TOLSTOY AT REST

From a Painting by Repin

had finished all her
her apparatus, with
ground

began to urge the players to
later, a company of twelve
across the park. Lyeff Niko-
expedition. We went up hill
way through the thicket, crossed
plank. Lyeff Nikolaevitch
and talkative; he helped the
and even invented for one lady
an elevator: he pressed
the back of her belt, and

bow-

dark green
against the garden
We turned aside
them, and took
highway. Lyeff Niko-
everything, entered into
exchanged friendly
we met, without wait-
In all, we traversed about
end of the walk, all felt

in the dining-room.
Lyeff Nikolaevitch
de Paris, which he
It is a genuine

luxury for him to half recline, after a good walk, with a new book in his hands.

Evening began to draw on. Candles were brought to the tea-table. On the other, the round table, which stood in the corner, a lamp with a shade was placed. Sophia Andreevna laid out to dry the photographs which she had taken during the day, and then took up her sewing, and seated herself at the round table, bending low over her work. She always has some work on hand, and is constantly making or making over something for Lyeff Nikolaevitch, or for her youngest daughter, or for some of the house-servants. The elder daughters departed to their own rooms. The youngest, eleven-year-old Sasha, sat by the table, and played chess with a Gymnasium lad who had arrived. Two little boys in every-day blouses played battledore and shuttlecock, urging each other on with expressions of the most insulting description for the pride of the player, of this sort: "You, sir, ought to be playing with dolls still, instead of at battledore and shuttlecock." "You, señor, ought to learn first, how to hold your battledore, and then you might make up your mind to play with people who —" and so forth.

The large hall, with its dark squares of ancient portraits, was submerged in semi-obscurity. Several objects melted into their outlines. In the corners the plaster busts of Lyeff Nikolaevitch shone white, — one the work of the painter Gay, the other by I. Ryépin. Near the wall was the long, dark silhouette of the grand piano, with the uncertain outlines of the music piled upon it, and of the *balaláika*[1] and the mandolin. On the tables everywhere were books, journals, illustrations.

Suddenly brisk, shuffling steps became audible, and, creaking up the stairs, Lyeff Nikolaevitch hastily entered the room with the French magazine in his hand. His face was excited.

"What horrors are being perpetrated in Turkey! Heavens, and when will all this end? Tanya, Masha,

[1] A three-stringed musical instrument. — Tr.

come here. Hearken to what is going on in Armenia," said Lyeff Nikolaevitch, so loudly that he could be heard two rooms off.

The games ceased. Lyeff Nikolaevitch's two eldest daughters made their appearance in the hall. All seated themselves around the table with the lamp, and Lyeff Nikolaevitch began to read about the Sassoon horrors, interrupting his reading with various remarks, in order to control the emotion which overpowered him. Lyeff Nikolaevitch reads superbly. But dramatic scenes are beyond his powers. As he possesses remarkably acute artistic feeling, he seems to divine the approaching horror of the drama a whole verst off, and his voice, in spite of himself, becomes oppressed.

The description of the Sassoon brutalities produced a profound impression on all. As he read several scenes, Lyeff Nikolaevitch threw himself back from the book, and said: —

"How terrible this is!"

For some time the conversation hovered about the massacre at Sassoon. The servant brought the mail, which, however, produces no sensation here, because it is received from three stations, and always in abundance. A whole bundle of letters, notifications, and telegrams were addressed to Lyeff Nikolaevitch. He opens them, lays some on one side, leaves others, and reads some aloud, when, if the letter is written in any foreign language, in the presence of guests it is immediately read in Russian, with only a few pauses.

A German journalist writes to Lyeff Nikolaevitch a fervent letter about one of his articles. K., an Englishman, imparts from London a whole mass of political and literary news. The conversation turns upon English literature.

At ten o'clock the servants begin to set the table for supper. Although Lyeff Nikolaevitch has been speaking with animation, and has been courteous to all, something seems to have congealed in his face, and not a single note of cheerful tone now breaks forth from his voice.

He played a game of chess, but this did not distract his mind. During supper, loud voices became audible down-stairs, and new visitors made their appearance, good friends of the Tolstoys who had come from Moscow. They brought with them a whole budget of the most vitally interesting news. Lyeff Nikolaevitch was very glad to see his guests, and chatted with them in a friendly manner, but his face still wore an expression of dissimulation and sadness, as it were. The description of human suffering in Armenia had evidently left a painful sediment in his soul.

The next morning, various petitioners, male and female, began to make their appearance. From Tula came some officer or other, with a pale, nervous face, and after him, a lady in mourning garments. Lyeff Nikolaevitch received them, but the interviews did not last long, not more than a few minutes. Again, near the *poor people's tree*, peasants, passers-by, old men, and old women, with various petitions, were awaiting Lyeff Nikolaevitch. Again he did what he could for each one. Again the post brought a big pile of letters, newspapers, pamphlets, notifications, telegrams, with different requests, questions, and expectations.

After dinner, Lyeff Nikolaevitch rode into Tula on his bicycle, to see a friend.

Twilight began to descend. Several of us visitors were chatting together in the lower drawing-room which adjoins the library. Hasty steps became audible, and Lyeff Nikolaevitch entered. He bent forward, looked for an empty seat, and sat down with us. There was a peculiar warmth in his voice. This was not the famous Lyeff Tolstoy, the great writer and passionate preacher, but rather a gentle, modest Publican, conscious of his imperfections, and beholding before him, as yet, only the first steps of that lofty staircase which must be mounted.

In answer to his question, what were we talking about, one of us said that we had been discussing a family well known to all of us, in which discord was smoldering. Two of those present blamed the wife, and exculpated the husband. Lyeff Nikolaevitch listened attentively, and said:—

"But can we make all our demands on a woman, and judge her harshly, when we have ourselves trained her to all sorts of falsehood? Do we not prize in her, above all else, precisely that which relates to her sex, and do we not take her to wife because of that? And, all of a sudden, we demand that she shall be our *friend*. That is false, and a lie. I will seek a friend for myself among men. And no woman can take the place of my friend. Then why do we lie to our wives, and assure them that we regard them as our true friends? Surely, that is untrue."

"But what are we to do? How is peace to be established in a family?" asked one of us.

"The husband must take upon himself the *whole* burden of the false situation which he has created, and be indulgent to his wife," said Lyeff Nikolaevitch, with ardent conviction. "Never, under any circumstances, for any consideration whatever, should he deprive his wife of his support, because marriage is an elevation for the majority of such sinful men as we. When we choose for our wife a certain woman, we thereby, as it were, announce to all the other women in the world they are *our sisters*. Therein lies the profound meaning of marriage. But if any one can remain virgin, without distorting his nature, that must be a lofty happiness!"

And Lyeff Nikolaevitch told us that he knew one married pair, who had lived together many years, observing between them the relations of brother and sister. The daily equality of their relations always charmed Lyeff Nikolaevitch to such a degree, that one day he wrote them a friendly letter, in which he congratulated the wife with especial warmth upon the purity of these relations. To this letter he received an unexpected reply, which, nevertheless, touched him profoundly. She wrote him that, in spite of all her delight over his letter, she must, nevertheless, decline all his praises, because the most cherished desire of her heart was to be, not the friend, but *the wife of her husband*, and to have children by him, but that her husband wished to maintain chaste relations with her, therefore be it according to his will.

At these words, Lyeff Nikolaevitch's voice broke, and he wept.

"Which of us sinners," said he, conquering his emotion, "would dare to reproach them if, after all, they should come together as husband and wife? But that frank confession from the mouth of a modest woman, and her tranquil obedience to her husband's will — how beautiful it all is!"

And Lyeff Nikolaevitch continued for a long time still to discuss the moral side of marriage.

His ardent faith in the triumph of the highest principles in man, his profound belief in the vivifying power of moral ideals, an inspiration wherein is concealed also the deepest significance of our life, and the most healing remedy for all ills, in short, that peculiar, entrancing Tolstoy tone, which, like a tightly stretched chord, resounds in some of his writings, — all this here, in the twilight, in the intimate, low-voiced conversation, when every word acquires its special language, had a particularly attractive power.

When we were called to tea, and went up-stairs, as we mounted the stairs we experienced a sensation as though our wings had begun to grow. And our earthly burdens did not seem to us very heavy.

And that whole memorable evening afterward assumed a sort of peculiarly elegiac character. Several of us took our departure at twelve o'clock at night, and we felt sad at leaving that roof, beneath which we had lived through so many never-to-be-forgotten impressions.

After tea a general conversation arose about music, poetry, and verses. One of Tolstoy's feminine relatives read, in a peculiar, drawling elocution, several new-fashioned poems in the symbolical style, "with lilac sounds," and "gnawing perfumes." Lyeff Nikolaevitch stood by the piano, with his hand thrust into the belt of his blouse, and listened, with a smile, to the reading. When it was over, he laughed, and said: —

"Well, if it is a question of taking into your mouth all the sonorous words, and then letting them out again, you had better read Fet. In him there is both poetry and taste."

And, raising his head a little, as though trying to recall something half-forgotten, Lyeff Nikolaevitch recited, with much expression, one of Fet's poems, in which the poet compares the starry sky to an overturned urn.

We began to talk about Fet.

Countess Sophia Andreevna tried to recall one of his poems dedicated to her, and set to music, but was unable to do so.

Lyeff Nikolaevitch seated himself at the piano, and with a free, light touch, played that romance. Tatyana Lvovna, the eldest daughter of the Tolstoys, approached the piano in a flowered peasant woman's jacket, and asked her father if he would not accompany her. He gladly consented. She took up her mandolin, leaned against the piano, and they began to play harmoniously and melodiously, presenting an enviable group for an artist.

After the music, Lyeff Nikolaevitch approached his guests, and chatted in a friendly manner with each one of those who were about to depart. At eleven o'clock, the *katki* — that is, a long jaunting-car which will hold ten persons — drove up to the door.

The night was clear and cool. The whole Tolstoy family came out on the porch to wish the parting guests God-speed.

When the katki drove away from the house, all, as though at a given signal, turned round, and gazed long through the dense grove at the lighted windows of the long house in which had flowed past the greater part of the extremely active life of one of the most remarkable men in the history of mankind.

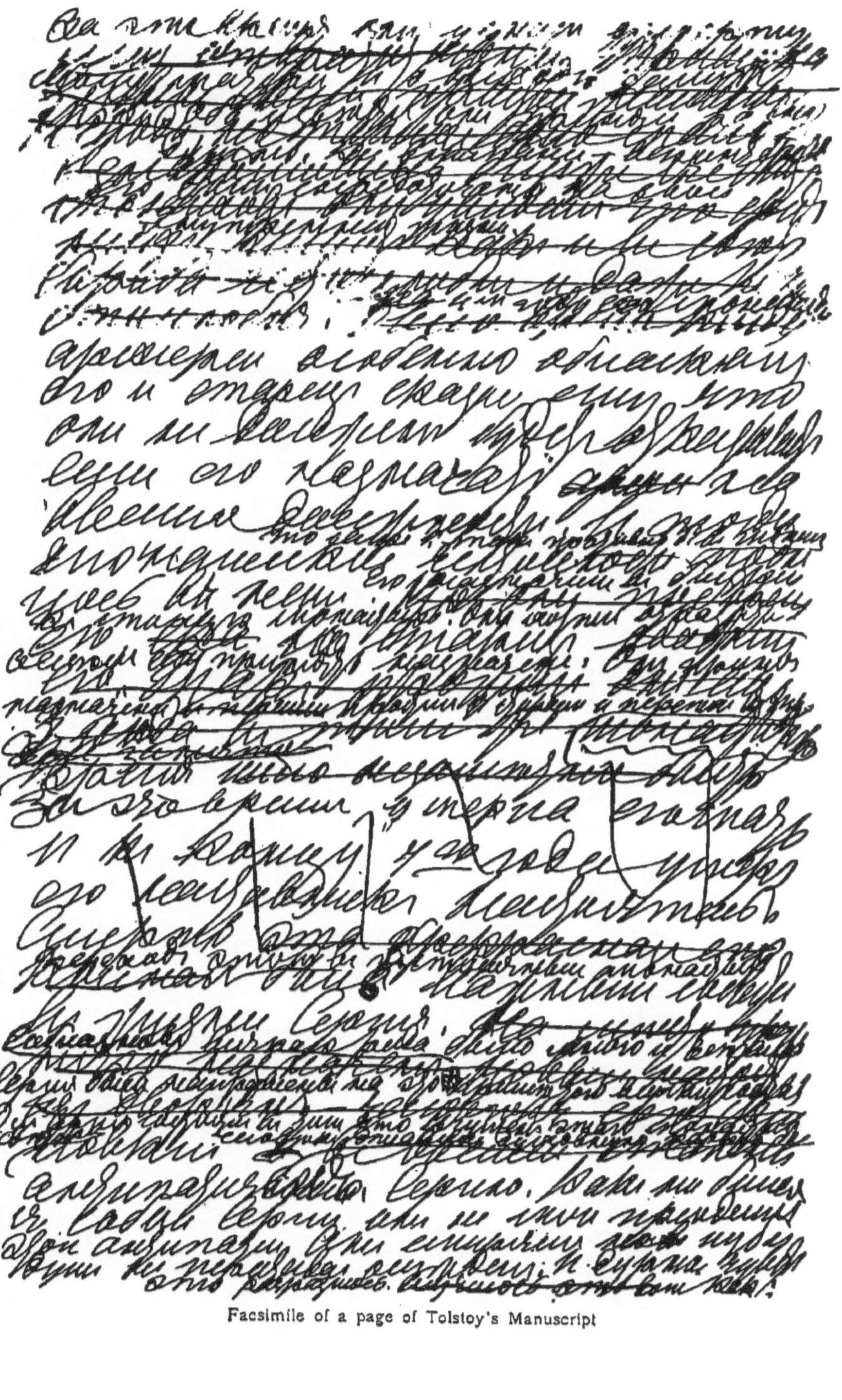

Facsimile of a page of Tolstoy's Manuscript

www.ingramcontent.com/pod-product-compliance
Lightning Source LLC
Chambersburg PA
CBHW032016010726
47493CB00007B/2433
9783337319526